WITHDRAWN

# MOVING ON

*by*

Millie Gray

HIGHLAND
LIBRARIES

170005195

**Magna Large Print Books**
Long Preston, North Yorkshire,
BD23 4ND, England.

British Library Cataloguing in Publication Data.

A catalogue record of this book is
available from the British Library

ISBN 978-0-7505-4482-5

First published in Great Britain 2016 by
Black & White Publishing Ltd.

Copyright © Millie Gray 2016

Cover illustration © Ildiko Neer/Arcangel by arrangement with
Arcangel Images Ltd.

The right of Millie Gray to be identified as the author of this work has
been asserted by her in accordance with the Copyright, Designs and
Patents Act, 1988

Published in Large Print 2017 by arrangement with
Black & White Publishing Ltd.

All rights reserved. No part of this publication may be reproduced,
stored in a retrieval system, or transmitted in any form or by any
means, electronic, mechanical, photocopying, recording or otherwise
without the prior permission of the Copyright owner.

Magna Large Print is an imprint of Library Magna Books Ltd.

Printed and bound in Great Britain by
T.J. (International) Ltd., Cornwall, PL28 8RW

This novel is a work of fiction. The names, characters and incidents portrayed in it are of the author's imagination. Any resemblance to actual persons, living or dead, events or localities is entirely coincidental.

*For Diane Cooper for her assistance when all appeared to be lost. Also I have to thank my sister Mary Gillon for her support and Diane Cooper for her first edit of the book and all the staff at Black & White for their help, expertise and encouragement.*

# PART ONE

## MAY 1945

Johnny Anderson wasn't aware of the three little tearaways careering along the Leith Links road until one of them bumped into his left side. The sudden, unexpected impact caused Johnny to stagger and reel. In an effort to regain his balance he immediately placed his right hand over his elbowed stump – the upper stump that was all that remained of his left arm.

'Och, Jimmy,' one of the laddies blustered, 'can you no see the man's a wounded sodger. No got a hand, so he hasnae.' The lad stopped and spat before adding, 'Probably had it blown clean aff by a grenade in the war.'

Jimmy sniffed and wiped under his nose with his fingers. 'Sorry, mister, but dinnae you worry cause ye cannae be hurt nae mair.'

'Aye, that's right,' the only girl in the trio chanted. 'Listen, mister, can you no hear the bells? Ringing aw day they hae been to tell us that it's aw ower. Aye, the war's aw ower!'

'That's right, Rena. And ken this, mister,' Alec added as he nudged Johnny's right arm, 'we're on our way to the street parties. Are you going to one?' Johnny stayed mute so Alec winked before continuing, 'See you being a wounded sodger will mean you'll get the pick of the sandwiches and as

9

many sausage rolls and jellies and ice creams as you want.'

Chuckling, Johnny replied, 'Like you I'm glad it's all over. By the way what's your names?'

'I'm the biggest, I'm ten and my name is Alec Ross. Rena's ma wee sister and Jimmy he's ten tae, but he doesnae act it. Our mammy says he's no the full shilling so we *hae* to be kind to him and let him tag along.'

Johnny smiled. 'And when the three of you grow up what are you going to be?'

Alec huffed. 'My ma says I havnae to be like my dad and I've tae get aff my bahookie. That means I'll probably hae to get a job in the docks.'

'Your ma doesnae say bahookie, she says to your dad to get aff his ar...'

'Okay,' Alec spat, 'but we're no allowed to say anything but bahookie ... are we?'

Jimmy just nodded.

'Don't know if getting a job in the docks will be all that easy,' Johnny slowly drawled.

'Will be for me, mister, you see my uncle works there, and he'll speak up for me.'

Johnny smiled and nodded. That was certainly how things worked before the war. But now? He sighed before allowing a wicked smile to play on his lips as he acknowledged that with the winds of change blowing in a new and more just order, who knew what would happen?

'And, mister,' Rena said, pulling on Johnny's trouser pocket to get his attention, 'I want to be a teacher but my mammy says I'll be like her and only be allowed into Moray House Teachers' College to scrub the flairs.' Rena then sighed long and hard before adding, 'You see, you hae to be a toff to be a teacher and we're skint and bide in Sleigh Drive ... so there's nae hope of me getting to teach.'

Johnny chuckled, but before he could reply, the children heard the music that was drifting over from several of the Leith Links street parties and they scampered off. As he watched them hurtle over the greens, he allowed his amusement to be replaced by deep contemplation – he was thinking about the aspirations the country had for the future. So deep was he in his ponderings that he was unaware that a number thirteen bus had drawn level with him until the driver, Joe Armstrong, shouted, 'Here, Johnny, do you want a free hurl up Restalrig Road?'

Johnny shook his head. 'Naw, Joe. I'm just going to dander up and maybe join in one or two of the festivities.'

Truth was Johnny wanted to reflect – have time on his own to think back.

The declaration of war, on 3rd September 1939, between Britain and Germany, and the subsequent bombings of Leith, had not had the devastating effect on Johnny that his home circumstances had.

He became so immersed in these personal recollections that he had crossed over Vanburgh Place and was ambling up Restalrig Road when he began to be swamped by those poignant memories – memories so painful that he had to stop and lean against the licensed grocer's shop window for support. Without warning he suddenly convulsed

11

in sobs as he recalled his family's personal events of 1939.

That was the year when his beautiful and vivacious wife Sandra whispered in his ear that she, at the age of thirty-seven, was pregnant again. He remembered that Saturday afternoon so well because they seemed to be nineteen or twenty again and had just discovered that their first child, Bobby, was on his way. They could not have been happier, and yes the country was now at war, but the hostilities all seemed so far away in Europe that they could not believe they would have any effect on them or their contentment and well-being.

Unfortunately, bombs that burst out of the blue, either real or figurative, cause mayhem and devastation. The ravages, however, are not only felt in the original crater but also in the surrounding areas. Innocent people become swamped by the shock waves, and the merciless fallout. These consequences were no more true than when thirty-seven-year-old Sandra died giving birth to Rosebud. The catastrophic effects from this blast not only affected Johnny but it changed, for the worse, the life of Kitty, pretty Kitty, his bubbly fifteen-year-old daughter. The poor girl, who had so much promise, found herself no longer continually crossing then uncrossing her perfect legs whilst taking her boss's dictation and then expertly typing up his letters – no, she grudgingly became 'Mother' to fractious Rosebud and unpaid housekeeper for her father's household.

Johnny's reveries then shifted to his son, Jack. Consequently he felt the need to pull himself away from the shop window and stand erect in reverence. A right 'Jack the Lad' his twenty-year-old son had been. He sighed long and hard as he acknowledged that he never ever would come to terms with his ship being torpedoed in the Mediterranean. The loss of Jack was another bomb blast that had knocked him sideways. He nodded as he accepted that it was against nature for a father to mourn the loss of his child. Life, he conceded, was unfortunately like what the Bible promised – oh aye, every life would receive its share of the good years and the bad. Johnny from experience knew that this was true, and how. He also knew that he continually tried to reason and justify why the good and just God, that he worshipped, could take the life of a carefree charmer like his son Jack – a lad who was just stepping out onto the world's stage – a lad who had just finished his apprenticeship and was eager to do his bit in the war whilst he sailed the seven seas – and still even today, as the victory bells were ringing out, the answer eluded him.

Johnny was now biting so hard on his bottom lip that he drew blood – warm salty blood that dribbled down his chin. Lifting his hand to wipe away the trickling stream he admitted that the discomfort from his self-inflicted wound was easy to thole. So much easier than the relentless agony of wondering if his selfish actions of bedding and marrying Connie had somehow driven Jack to join the Merchant Navy and then be lost to him forever. Thinking back to the passing of Jack saw Johnny curling his right hand into a vice-like grip. This was because he felt he had to inflict pain on

13

himself to atone for any wrong he may have done.

He was just about to berate himself further when the familiar voice of his longtime workmate and confidant Jock brought him back to consciousness. 'What was that you said, Jock?' he mumbled.

'Just wondering, so I am, if you're lashing yourself again?' Johnny shook his head. 'Well that will be a first. So that leaves me wondering if you're going up the brae and home to your bonnie lassies or can I tempt you back to the Links Tavern for a double victory dram?'

Johnny hunched his shoulders and contemplated for a minute. 'A double dram it is because we have things to discuss.'

Jock nodded and smiled when Johnny gave him a friendly pat on the shoulder.

Meanwhile at Leith Hospital the young, handsome and dashing Canadian doctor grabbed hold of Sister Jean Duff and began waltzing her around the children's ward. This spontaneous spectacle resulted in the children who were able, to jump up and dance around their cots.

Anderson and Keane, the two second-year – so judged to be senior – probationer nurses did try to quieten the children but both collapsed against a cot as their efforts to suppress and control their laughter failed.

'Doctor McNeill,' shrieked a highly indignant Sister Duff, as she disentangled herself from his arms, 'may I remind you that this is an establishment for healing not ... reeling.'

Undeterred Dougal grabbed the sister again. 'I

know that. But listen, Jeanie, the bells, the bells are ringing out to tell us it's over. The bloody war is over ... all over.'

Jean, eyes bulging, nose snorting, knees buckling, pushed against Dougal in an effort to escape his hold. 'It may be, Doctor McNeill,' she panted and spluttered, when she eventually managed to extricate herself from his grasp, 'that the war in Europe is over but let me inform you that the war in here,' she gasped again, 'against disease and pestilence goes on.'

Dougal's response was to lunge towards Jean again. But before he could recapture her she, in absolute panic, fled swiftly on her hobbling legs from the ward. She had just catapulted herself through the swing doors when, as luck would have it, she careered into Matron.

With a look of complete disdain, which she had spent many years perfecting, Matron hissed, 'Sister Duff, you are not in uniform.' Jean looked up but said nothing. 'Please straighten your cap and where, might I ask, is your right shoe?' Sister Duff could only sniff and shake her head so in clipped tones Matron continued, 'Decorum. Oh yes, sister, decorum by senior staff must be observed at all times.'

Back in the ward, to the delight of the children, who were still shaking their cots, an over-exuberant Dougal McNeill was now dancing a protesting Dotty Keane up the ward.

'Whoa, whoa!' Kitty exclaimed. 'Look here's Matron coming and by the look on her face, we're all for it.'

Dougal drew up so quickly that Dotty toppled

over and slithered directly into the path of Matron.

Matron's face convulsed before it turned all the colours of the rainbow. Then, snorting like an overheated dragon, she looked contemptuously down at Dotty before hissing, 'Keane, what on earth do you think you are doing? Have you *no* regard for the welfare of your young patients?'

By now Dougal had squeezed past Matron, and Kitty could only look on in dismay at his fleeing figure. 'Matron, madam,' she spluttered, 'Doctor McNeill was just...'

'Just what?'

'Just that he ... and I'm sure he didn't mean to but he did get a bit overexcited about the war being over.'

Matron continued to glower before announcing, 'I am just going to go over to the children's surgical ward and when I return,' she glanced down at her fob watch before adding, 'in *exactly* five minutes, I expect you, Keane, to be up off the floor, and to see this ward being run as it should be, Anderson.'

Two freshly-drawn pints had just been set down in front of the two pals when Jock said, 'You seem a bit put out. What I mean is you look as if someone has stolen your tattie scone.'

Johnny bit on his lip and then made a few clucking sounds before replying, 'Well if someone coming into your patch and walking away with your dream counts as your scone getting nicked then I am cheesed off.'

'What are you going on about?'

16

'Just that the selection committee for the election ... which by the way is less than two months away...'

'They've set the date already?'

'Aye, and would you believe it is to be 5th July this year!' Jock frowned. Johnny now adopted a long-suffering expression before adding, 'But back to what's bugging me ... have they no just handed the candidacy for Leith to a foreigner.'

'What foreigner?'

'That Jimmy Hoy bloke.'

Jock chuckled before taking a long slurp from his pint. 'Hoy's no a foreigner,' he then replied. 'Sure the lad was born in Edinburgh. Educated at Causewayside and Sciennes corporation schools, so he was.'

'That's what I mean,' Johnny spat. 'He's from above the Leith boundary line and here's me that has slaved all my days in the Leith shipyards and stood up for the working men there and I've been kicked into touch.'

'Are you saying that after all we've done to get you noticed that you didnae get a shot at a seat?'

'Cannae exactly say that,' Johnny huffed.

'You cannae?'

'Naw, because, right enough, I've been handed the chance to bring hame a victory in the Wider Granton one.'

Jock shook his head. 'Get a grip, Johnny.'

'What do you mean?'

'Just that you're lucky to be getting a chance to fight for a seat in the election. And okay it's no going to be as easy a seat to win as Leith would be but if you put in enough effort you can still

17

bring home a victory.'

'That remains to be seen. Besides I wanted to stand for Leith ... my industrial hame. It's where I'm known for doing my best for the workers and their families. I'm one of them.'

'Aye, but "Hoy's the boy" is the best guy to send that Devonshire Liberal boy, Ernest Brown, back to England to think again.'

'How could I have no done that?'

'Forget it. And you will win Granton and hands down at that. What you have to do is get to know your voters.'

'Oh aye, I can see myself banging on the doors of Davidson's Mains and asking if they will vote for Labour and them replying aye, son, just as soon as I have stopped counting my money.'

'Look. I'm no half glad you weren't at Dunkirk.'

'What do you mean?'

'Well with your attitude we would never have got the men off the blinking beaches.'

'Are you saying I'm a defeatist?'

'No. You're saying that about yourself.' Jock slurped from his pint again. Before he continued he nudged Johnny playfully. 'But I ken you can win Wider Granton. All you have to do is stop sulking and start thinking about all you have going for you...'

'Like what?'

'Your family and pals like me that will be knocking on the doors along with you.'

Johnny grunted before a sly smile broke on his face. 'Have I to start right away or do you think we have time for another pint?'

'Well as it's your round ... pints it needs to be.'

Johnny's twenty-year-old daughter, Kitty, was nursing a cup of steaming weak tea in Lanny's café in Henderson Street when she looked up at the window and saw Doctor Dougal making faces at her.

In feigned disgust, she shrugged and looked away. However, he ignored her rebuff and bounced jauntily into the café. He then threw himself down on the bench beside her. Immediately she tried to put space between them but whenever she did he snuggled up closer to her until the wall prevented her from escaping his advances.

'You've got a nerve,' she hissed before banging her cup down.

'Is that so?' He just laughed, whilst leaning forward to tickle her chin. Her response was to brusquely brush his hand away. She then found herself squirming as she thought, *Why does this man disturb me so? Why am I so pleased to be sitting so close beside him, so close that I can smell that he has recently been smoking his pipe? That blooming pipe, whose lingering wholesome aroma of his Caledonian Mixture Tobacco, has my stomach feeling as if it has been invaded by a swarm of fluttering butterflies.*

Trying to control her emotions she inhaled deeply. Her eyes then became fixed on him as he fumbled in his pockets to bring out his pipe and tobacco tin. As the exotic aroma of the Virginia tobacco wafted over her she began to feel like an overexcited, bewitched teenager. Willingly inhaling the exotic scent she became as if hypnotised and she mumbled, 'How much does that tobacco cost?'

He was now puffing deeply sending more of the redolence over to her and around the room. 'This,' he said tapping the tin 'costs a whole one shilling and three pence per ounce and if you are thinking of treating me you can get it from the tobacco shop at the foot of Leith Walk.'

This impertinent retort brought Kitty down from cloud nine and she countered his insolence with, 'Me ... buy you tobacco? With the carry on you had on the ward today the only thing I would be happy to buy you is a one-way ticket for the next ship sailing for Canada!'

He chortled as he leaned in and elbowed her. 'Come on, you're just mad that I didn't dance you around the ward. Admit it, you like me being a bit of a lad who doesn't exactly follow the rules...'

'Doesn't exactly follow the rules ... you don't know what a rule is.'

'Yes I do. And I am going to observe one right now and ask you to go out to the pictures with me and if you say yes I won't make eyes at anyone else until they play "God Save the King".'

Before Kitty could reply there was a loud rap on the window and they both looked up to see that Audrey Skillon – the shameless self-appointed forces sweetheart – was attempting to get Dougal's attention.

The sight of Audrey sensuously winking at Dougal caused Kitty to flop against the bench back. This girl, she thought, was not the usual type to be training in Leith Hospital. Oh no, and according to Matron, nurses and probationer nurses were as close as you could get to being referred to as 'ladies'. Kitty inwardly laughed as she remembered that she was told that Matron had said that as far as she was concerned Audrey Skillon was no Florence Nightingale. In fact, she thought that she was the nearest you could get to being a 'Lili Marlene' and therefore should never have been allowed to don a nurse's uniform, especially a Leith Hospital one.

Kitty didn't know why she instinctively put her arm through Dougal's before whispering, 'I'm free after early shift tomorrow and there's a James Mason film showing at the Palace Picture House.'

Dougal beamed and kissed Kitty on the cheek before raising his hand to dismiss a piqued Audrey.

Kate sat twisting her gold wedding ring. The ring that up to a year ago she thought she would never wear, and then out of the blue, Hans, a Polish refugee, had come into her life. She hunched her shoulders and sucked in a long breath before she allowed her shoulders to relax and sink down. Continuing to breathe deeply she willingly allowed her mind to picture Hans' long gifted fingers – the skilful fingers that had so lovingly repaired her father's granddaughter clock.

Raising her head she now had a full view of the clock. Running her tongue over her lips she remembered that when the clock had crashed to the floor from the force of a nearby bomb blast, she had wept so sorely. Picking up the bits she had thought that it was beyond repair. But Hans, with his skilful, sensitive hands, had accomplished the impossible, and there the clock stood ticking away the seconds of their lives.

Sinking back into her chair Kate thought again about the power that Hans' gentle hands had. She gave a delicious sigh as she remembered that not only had these hands brought back life to the clock but also to herself. Until then she, and everyone else, had considered herself, as a dried-up, emotionless old spinster. She smiled and softly exhaled as she revelled in her recollections. It was true that when she reached forty she still wore no wedding ring but she had known love. Young love – the rash desperate love of two young people who somehow know that because of a cruel and senseless war their one night of passion was all that they would ever have. When faced with remembering 1915 Kate always wrapped her arms tightly around herself as if somehow trying to keep the cruel world of war out and something precious inside herself safe. But what she tried to keep safe, a baby – her and Hugh's unborn baby – was not to be. No, when she tumbled down the Leith Provident department store attic stairway her mother was saved the embarrassment of telling the world that her fifteen-year-old unmarried daughter was pregnant. She sighed as she accepted that was good for her mother – her dear mother, who would not have deserved that humiliation. But the downside for herself was that her chance of being a mother, nursing her own child, had rolled away forever when she'd rolled down and down that rickety staircase.

Without thinking, she unwound her arms from around herself. She then began sucking on her thumb and acknowledged that she owed a debt of gratitude to her brother, who had fathered a large family which he had always shared with her. But that was not the same as having your own. Hans had had children but they had perished with his wife in the merciless Warsaw blitz. Why she wondered did Hans never talk of his children and why hadn't she told him about Hugh and losing her baby? And she argued, with herself, that if they were as happy and secure in their love for each other, as they thought they were, why were they not completely honest with each other? Why, oh why, was she thinking about all this now?

To be honest, she had no need to think about why she was looking back. It was so obvious. Yes, she had lost count of the many times that Hans had mentioned in the last few months that he would like to find out if anyone he had known in Poland had miraculously survived the Holocaust – and yet he never ever suggested his wife or children. Perhaps the reason for that omission was that it would have been too painful for him to imagine that any of them had survived the Warsaw Blitz and then have to endure the barbaric treatment and conditions of the concentration camps.

What Kate did know was that the news of the plight of the orphaned Jewish children was deeply disturbing to Hans. Every night he would say, 'Surely there are some families here in Scotland that could offer one or two of them a home.' Hans being completely fixated on these children's difficulties made Kate anxious and perplexed – after all, what did she know of Hans' life in Poland? Giving the matter serious thought she concluded

– nothing. Reluctantly she now wondered why he had never ever confided to her any of the details of his life before he had met her.


## HANS' STORY

The gold pocket watch that Hans was repairing wasn't getting his full attention. To be truthful it required only a clean and service. He had told the lady so when she had brought it in. She had then gone on to explain that her husband had been reluctant to take the family heirloom to war and now that he would be coming home she just wanted to be sure that the timepiece was in full working order.

In a dreamlike trance Hans continued to buff the gold casement whilst he became engulfed in guilt. The newsreels showing the inhuman fate that had befallen his people, whose only sin in Hitler's eyes was to be born Jewish, haunted his every living hour. Six million of his country people, three million of them Jews, had been slaughtered in the last five years. He tried to eat but the eyes of the starving Jewish children who had survived caused nausea to rise up in his throat and made swallowing just so difficult.

His thoughts then shifted to wondering why he was the only member of his immediate family to be spared. Had he, he continued to wonder, any right to forget his loving wife, children and friends and go on to be as blissfully happy as he was here in Leith?

Vividly he recalled how he and his cousin, Josef, had fled with four others in a dilapidated fishing boat. To their shame they had not even stayed long enough to dig in the rubble for their kinfolk's remains – not one had they seen into their final resting place. Most people would forgive this selfishness because they had to leave immediately or risk being captured by the advancing German troops. Their fate then would have been execution or worse.

On landing on the south coast of England, Josef, a young nineteen-year-old bachelor, had decided to stay and enlist in the British Army and continue the fight against the Nazis from there. Hans was tempted to do the same but, to his shame, the will to go on living had been knocked out of him. He really just wanted to curl up and die. To be truthful it was Josef who had pulled him away from Warsaw. 'Hans,' he had said, 'you are all that is left of my close and wider family. There is nothing and nobody left here. We cannot win by staying here but we can go to England and continue the fight from there.' It had been as if in a trance that Hans had agreed. He did, at that time, wish to tear the hearts out of the invaders with his bare hands and trample them into the dust, but now...?

He looked down at the gleaming watch again. He sighed. Yes, it was true that on arrival in Leith, and he would never know what made him decide to seek refuge in Leith, he had taken a job just cleaning and portering in the Leith Provident department store. At the time he started there that was all he was capable of doing. It was there that the numbness of his inconsolable grief began to slowly thaw. Oh yes, ever so slowly he began to feel human again. He smiled as he recalled how it was Kate, his now beloved Kate, a mature woman who worked as a manager in the department store, who had awakened those feelings again. Gradually, steadily, they had fallen in love and being with her had helped to heal the terrible psychological wounds that he had imagined were incurable.

From the day he had escaped Poland until the day he took Kate as his lawful wife, he had always thought he would never know true happiness and contentment again. But on that wonderful wedding day he did. Oh yes, when he began his new life with his lovely Kate, he truly believed that Poland and its ghosts had been well and truly laid to rest forever. But as the war in Europe drew to its close and the horrific news filtered out about the inhuman treatment of the Jews by the Nazis – Poland, the land of his birth and his fellow countrymen seemed to be calling him – asking him, begging him – to help them. It was these perceived entreaties that had taken him every day, and sometimes twice a day, in the last three months into the Palace Picture House next door.

The head usherette would let him in the back door so he could watch just the newsreels. The grotesque, cruel photographic evidence, along with the oral commentary, held him rooted to the spot. He really didn't wish to see what had happened to his people but there was some innate feeling that told him he had to be made aware of the fate of his countrymen. This vexed him as he had tried so hard to keep Poland and all his memories of it buried deeply within his subconscious. But, and again it was a very big but, he now knew Poland and his past life there would never ever allow him to forget. It was determined always to remain in his subconscious ready to jump into his mind's eye to torment and accuse him. Always his thoughts of Poland made him feel guilty that he had escaped the worst of the atrocities and now lived a comfortable life – a life of milk and honey compared to those in the concentration camps. He unconsciously moaned. Unaware that he was buffing the watch case again he thought of how when he arrived home there would always be the smell of home cooking. Oh yes, the house in Parkvale Place was clean and bright, but never could you say that it was sanitized – it was a home. A home where he was welcome – a home where within its walls he became so comfortable that he never wished to leave – never wished to be anywhere but within its safety. It was a place where he could fool himself into thinking that this was how the world was for everybody now and not how it really was for...

Memories flooded in on him. Memories of the privileged life he had led in Warsaw. He ran the buffing cloth over his long, sensitive fingers. These fingers that from an early age he had been were gifted to him so that he could create beautiful things – lovingly restore artefacts back to their original splendour. It was these fingers that had opened Kate's heart to him. Always he would remember the look on her face when she gazed upon her father's granddaughter clock that he had restored to its original beauty.

The cloth slipped from his hand. He was in a world of his own wondering why he had never told Kate about his contented home life in Poland. Somehow he felt it was because he was afraid. Terrified he was to actually mouth the words of how happy he had been until that fateful day in 1939 when Hitler decided to invade his beloved country. How could he confide to Kate that his childhood had been idyllic? That he was just into adulthood when he met his wife and they had fallen deeply in love then had married and had three such beautiful and talented children. His eldest son took after himself, a gentle boy, who loved nature and his fellow man. Even now, Hans could close his eyes and the beautiful, melodic music that his son's nimble fingers coaxed out of their piano washed over him and filled him with overwhelming nostalgia. These times of yearning always seemed to be in the early evening after supper when his new family were all at home safe and happy. There was a desire to confess all his past life in detail to Kate but he was afraid that if he did tell her, and she could hear from his voice how the love for his wife and his children was still so very real and important to him, that somehow she would see it as a threat to herself. The magic spell that was still cast around them would then be broken.

He stood up and stretched. Reluctantly he acknowledged that Kate and he had become selfish – and very much so at that. They had built a cocoon around themselves where there was just room for the two of them. Up until now they seemed not to notice the outside world and its problems. Hans shuddered. He accepted that now he must tell Kate in detail about his family and in doing so risk bringing their honeymoon period to an abrupt end. Indeed, he knew that knowing Kate as he did, she would wrongly feel that she was a poor substitute for all he had lost.

He also knew himself very well. All his life he restored things that had become broken. That was why he couldn't comprehend why the Nazis had to destroy everything. But wasn't it strange that they did not succeed and there were people, buildings, precious objects that had survived and required loving, patient restoration? He could do nothing else but answer their compelling call that he was now continually hearing with ever-rising urgency.

The tinkling of the shop doorbell brought his brooding to an end. And when the door opened he was just so pleased to see Kate standing there. In the short time that they had been married she just seemed to grow lovelier as each day passed. There was now a serenity and contentment about her and when she smiled at him he felt overcome by his love for her.

'Bet you're surprised to see me,' she teased as her tantalising smile lit up her face.

'I am.' He chuckled. 'And I am very pleased that you appear to have got over your bout of sickness.'

'Yes, I am so much better that I intend to go back to work tomorrow.'

Kate was now in the back room of the shop and as she filled the whistling kettle she called back, 'Hans, I ... what I mean is... I just have to talk to you about... Oh, Hans it is so important that we...' She hesitated and was just about to rejoin him in the front shop when the doorbell tinkled again.

29

This time in bounced Mrs McArthur the Palace Picture House usherette.

'Hans,' she shouted, 'thought you'd like to know that we have a new, up-to-date, newsreel in and it will be showing in five minutes. So you go through and see it and I will watch the shop. Is that the kettle I hear singing?'

'It is,' replied Kate. 'I was just going to make a pot of tea.'

'Good, because this is my tea break. And I need a cuppa to wash down my stale sandwiches.'

Kate was now looking quizzically at Hans. 'Eh...' Hans stuttered. 'Maryann here allows me to slip in to see the newsreels.'

'Why are you stuttering, Hans? There is nobody I know who would expect you not to be interested in what has happened to Poland.' Maryann now turned her attention to Kate. 'Poor soul that he is,' she began with a knowing nod of her head, 'has been sneaking in to see the newsreels since January when that Auschwitz camp in Poland was liberated by the Russians. Bloody scandal that was. See myself, I just couldnae look at it, so I couldnae. I mean how could onybody dae that to wee defenceless bairns?' Maryann paused before adding, 'Ken what they should dae? Round up all they Nazi sympathisers and gie them a year-long holiday in one those bloody awful concentration camps.'

Neither Kate nor Hans responded to Maryann so she just kept on holding court with herself. All Kate and Hans could do was gaze at each other and their stance spoke volumes. Kate was completely stunned. Why, she wondered did she not know that Hans was completely obsessed with the news that was coming out of Europe? Hans on the other hand felt like a naughty schoolboy who had just been discovered pinching some sweets.

'Well,' Maryann continued, 'you'd better be off, Hans, or you will miss the Pathé News ... remember it is only on for five minutes.'

This reminder from Maryann jolted Hans and without uttering a word he dashed from the shop.

'Right,' Maryann puffed, 'I've been wasting time too. So.' She now opened a brown paper bag from which she took out a couple of sandwiches. Offering one to Kate she continued, 'Just fish paste but it's Shippams and you can't get better than that.'

Kate shook her head. She always thought that the strong aroma from the jars of fish and meat pastes somehow seemed obnoxious. It was true that the war had made most people's appetites adventurous and they would try anything, but as her mother made her own potted meat, she had never had to resort to swallowing the likes of Maryann's delicacies.

The sickening smell from Maryann's sandwiches, which was washing over Kate, caused her to look away, especially when Maryann began to over-pack her mouth. She was further nauseated when Maryann spluttered, 'Here, Mrs Busek, see if you ever fancy a night at the flicks here wait until the big picture has started, rap on the back door, and I'll slink you in.' Kate shook her head. Undeterred, Maryann leaned in closely to Kate so she could hoarsely whisper, 'Honestly it works. That's how Hans gets in to see the newsreels.

31

Doesnae cost him a penny so it doesnae.'

Kate had now managed to perch herself up on Hans' stool. Troublesome emotions were swamping her. They were a mixture of anger and regret because her 'perfect world' where Hans and she hid nothing from each other was now proving to be nothing but a romantic myth. Sorrow began to engulf her when she accepted that Hans, her beloved Hans, had not felt secure enough in their relationship to confide in her – to trust her to understand. Begrudging gratitude to Maryann, a rough diamond if there ever was one, also flooded Kate. It was however galling to her that this woman had understood Hans' instinctive need to find out exactly what had happened to Poland, the land of his birth. Devastated Poland, the land where he had spent his infancy and then his formative and early adult years. And it was Maryann that Hans had turned to and not herself when he required help and understanding about the suffering that had been inflicted on innocent Poland. It also disturbed her to acknowledge that Maryann had unselfishly met Hans' desperate needs.

The doorbell tinkling caused Kate to slip off the stool but as she crossed over to the door she was disappointed to be met by the postman rather than Hans. Without acknowledging the man she accepted the letter that he offered her.

'Hmmm,' Maryann simpered as she squinted at the envelope. 'A blue letter? Hope it doesn't smell nice. Cause if it does,' she teased, 'it usually means it's a billet-doux from a...' She paused before sensuously adding, 'secret lover.'

Kate lifted the envelope to her nose and

breathed in deeply. 'Smells right enough,' she replied with a chuckle, 'but not of "Mischief Perfume" just smoked fish.'

'Ah, well that's all right then,' chanted Maryann whilst giving Kate a knowing nudge in the shoulder.

Before Kate could respond the door opened again and there stood Hans.

Kate's hand flew to her mouth. She didn't understand what had put him into such a state of shock. 'Darling, what's wrong?' she pleaded.

But Hans, unaware of anything that was going on, could only stare into space.

'Look, Mrs Busek,' Maryann began as she tried to push past Hans, 'I would like to stay and help you with poor Hans but I am on duty ... just skipped out to cover the shop for him. That's all I ever do.'

Kate nodded, and when Maryann was safely away from the shop, Kate sat Hans down before she locked the door and turned the 'open' sign to 'closed'.

It was well past the Anderson family teatime when Johnny, by now quite merry, arrived home.

'Mummy, Mummy,' screeched Rosebud as she hurled herself towards her father. 'It's Daddy. So can I now get a poke of chips from the chippie?'

'Careful, Rosebud,' Johnny cautioned as he attempted to unwrap her arms from around his legs.

'Dadadada,' gasped eleven-month-old Jackie as she toddled ungainly towards Johnny.

It was at times like this that Johnny most keenly mourned the loss of his left arm in an accident in

June of last year. Before then he could have held his two youngest children in his arms. Today he could only scoop up one ... but which one? If he lifted Rosebud, Connie, his wife of fifteen months, would take umbrage. She would, no doubt, think he was favouring Rosebud over their darling infant, Jackie. If he instinctively lifted baby Jackie then Rosebud would throw one of her famous tantrums. Johnny did regret that it was impossible to get Rosebud to understand that she wasn't playing second fiddle to a baby, a baby she had no intention of tolerating. This all being the case, Johnny thought that he had best play safe and he moved away from the children and turned towards Connie. However, when Connie spurned his advance, he was dumbfounded. He was further confused when she announced, 'Your tea's in the oven and don't moan that the lorne sausage is frizzled and dried up and the chips are limp and soggy. Both were cooked to perfection when you were supposed to be home for your tea.' She glanced up at the clock before adding, 'some two hours ago.'

Without another word, Connie retreated into the kitchen and retrieved Johnny's sorrowful looking supper from the oven. She then banged it forcefully down on the table. Johnny looked at it and shrugged. He was going to complain but there was something in Connie's stance that had him think the better of saying anything.

Rosebud, however, thought she had a right to say something. 'Daddy,' she began whilst drawing in her lips, 'you're lucky Connie didn't go' – she now gave an imitation of someone retching and vomiting – 'right into your porridge like she did

34

to mine this morning.'

Johnny was now looking at Connie. 'Well?'

'Well nothing,' she replied. 'And it is not my fault...' Connie sank down on a chair and began to weep.

Instinctively Johnny began to rub Connie's back. 'Come on now, lass,' he coaxed. 'It's just that you are in the change of life and when that happens women get all moody.'

Connie's head jolted upwards. 'Johnny, it is not the change of life that is bothering me, it's me giving life...' she stopped to sob and brush her hand under her nose '...to another bairn...' Johnny's jaw dropped and his eyes popped. Connie was now weeping uncontrollably and he hardly heard her when she spluttered, 'And I'm nearly forty!... Don't you realise I will be the talk of the street?'

Johnny really didn't care what the street's gossips would think. He was more concerned about what this could possibly mean for his dreams and ambitions. He then did what he normally did when he was faced with panic; he began to slowly whistle 'The Old Rugged Cross'.

'Aye, well may you whistle that but it is me that is up there on the one next to Him! And I haven't even had time to get my figure back after Jackie and here is me about to wiggle and waddle again.'

Johnny diplomatically stayed silent, but taking a covert look at Connie's figure, he could only agree that she hadn't got back into any kind of shape since Jackie's birth. To be truthful, Connie was never what you would call the perfect shape. She was voluptuous, cuddly and comfortable and just so easy to love. He grimaced when he accepted

35

that was probably the reason she was in the family way again. His next thought was to mollify the situation so he put his arms about her and whispered in her ear, 'Let's get the wee ones away to bed then you and I will sit down and have a talk.'

'What's there to talk about?'

'Plenty,' Johnny replied, shaking his head dolefully. 'Firstly we have to decide what we are going to do ... especially...'

He never got to finish what he was going to say because Rosebud started to scream, 'I'm not going to bed and I want a piece and jam.'

'You, young lady, are going to bed and right now at that. So through you go.'

Rosebud's response was to lift up her foot and kick her father in the shin. 'You little...'

'Shit ... that's what they say I am,' Rosebud hollered.

'Who calls you that?'

'Your mother,' Connie responded.

'My mother!' Johnny expounded with 'Huh, huh,' before continuing, 'Aye, most folks' mothers might but certainly not mine.' He mumbled, 'Huh, huh,' again before adding, 'Never ever would my mother ever use such language about a bairn ... especially one of her own.'

'No? Well when our Rosebud threw a humdinger of a paddy today because your mother didn't have a sweetie for her, and I suggested that her behaviour was because she was tired, your mother said, "I am sick and tired of people saying that Rosebud's appalling behaviour is because she is tired. If that was the case then you should just put her to bed. But as it isn't ... you will all have to get

36

around to realising she is nothing but a precocious, spiteful little shit!"'

Johnny's jaw was in freefall again. 'No, my mother would never have used such a word.'

Connie sighed and looked up at the ceiling. It was difficult for her to say to Johnny that there was another problem that he would have to address. Well, one that he and his sister Kate would have to face, and that was that there was something going far wrong with their mother, Jenny. Slowly she drawled, 'Johnny dear, your mum ... well there is something amiss.'

'Amiss!'

'Yes like, like ... her starting to swear and she does such queer things now like...'

Fear began to arise in Johnny and in an effort to stay in control he grabbed hold of Connie before roaring, 'Like what?'

'Well, well, well ... like...' Connie being Connie did not wish to worry Johnny so, hesitating, she took time to compose herself before quietly uttering, 'Like ... talking to your dead dad. And believe me when I say I can cope with that.' She then stopped and took time to inhale deeply. After counting inwardly to ten she then said, 'But, Johnny, today I was gasping for a cup of tea but we had run out of milk and your mum said she would go for a bottle.'

'So,' Johnny interrupted, 'what was wrong with that?'

'Nothing ... except that when she came back it was a bottle right enough of – Harvey's Bristol Cream Sherry.'

Kate and Hans had just crossed over the door of their Parkvale Place home when Kate insisted that Hans should just drop himself down into her father's old comfortable armchair.

'No. No,' he replied, 'I couldn't speak to you in the shop but the walk home has...'

Hans was of course referring to the way Kate had closed the shop early for the day. She had then taken a benumbed Hans by the hand and they had zigzagged their way home through the crowds.

Firstly they had pushed their way down Morton Street and then on through Leith Links. The strange thing was that Kate and Hans, who found such succour in their never-ending chats, hadn't uttered a single word to each other during the journey. It was as if each was putting off facing up to what had happened – and must happen.

Kate, although grateful to Maryann, felt undermined by her because she had seen Hans' need and had catered for it. Kate now knew that there was a pressing need for her and Hans to talk things over. She wanted him to know that she was here to listen to him – here to help him unburden himself, listen to what was troubling him. She already knew that he was most concerned about what had been mercilessly inflicted on Poland and his country folk but, she hesitated, what else was troubling him?

However, as urgent as the clearing of the air was she thought that it should not be done in Hans' shop or as they strolled among the merry-making throngs. The best location for it was here in the safety of Parkvale Place, their home. After all, Parkvale Place was the place they had first made love to each other and where Hans had asked her to marry him and share his life. The thrill and happiness she'd felt on the day he had asked her to be his wife was still as real today as it had been on that very day.

Hans, on the other hand, stayed silent because he was overloaded with guilt. Firstly, this feeling of remorse was because he had survived the war, not only in Poland, but also here in Leith. Secondly, he deeply regretted that he had tried to put into the past his very loving wife and children who had been so mercilessly killed – he now knew that this was an impossibility. The third thing that wrung his conscience was that he had married Kate and had found peace and contentment with her but he had never been truly honest with her. Never had he told her about his previously happy family life. 'Why,' he asked himself, 'have I never told my Kate the names of my loving wife, who had also loved me as she does, or my beautiful children?' He knew this omission was so very wrong because he had lost count of the times that he, with his arms still around a sleeping Kate, remembered them, longed for them, felt so bereft and cheated.

Breathing in deeply he acknowledged that his family memories were bad enough to bear but now that the Pathé newsreels were showing him in detail what had happened to the children of his wider family, friends and colleagues, it was all becoming so unbearable. Every day he watched these films and every day he had to suppress the mounting need to do something to assist those needy little survivors. It was now so very clear to him that he could never be truly happy again until he tried to relieve some of the suffering of even one or two of those abused, innocent children. Indeed, if he didn't do something, he knew that the ghosts of his own children would never ever allow him to know peace again.

The problem was how could he confide all that was bothering him to Kate and still have her believe that he had wooed and married her because he loved her, saw the beauty in her and not because she was able to give him, a penniless Polish refugee, a home and security.

Kate saying his name brought him out of his reflections. 'Yes, dear, what is it?' he mumbled.

Quietly but firmly she said, 'Hans, we have to talk.'

He nodded.

'Firstly ... why did you not tell me how upset you were about the newsreels...?' She hesitated before stressing, 'And since January at that.'

He nodded again but this time he sought her hands.

Her reaction was to place them behind her back. He shrugged. 'Of course you are right. I have not been as honest with you as I should have been. So get a chair and sit opposite me and I will tell you all about my family, my life in Poland and how I feel now and what I wish to do about it.'

Kate grew anxious, but she got a chair and sat down on it. Looking directly into Hans' eyes she became concerned as she could see that silent tears were now trickling down his face.

'Esther, dearest Esther,' he began wistfully, 'was my loving wife and she bore me three children.

The eldest, David.' He paused. 'We chose David as his name because ... it means beloved. Oh Kate, he was my beloved eldest son and he was just so talented.' Hans' tears were now drying and as he spoke of his family Kate could see that he still loved them and had so much pride in them. 'Our old piano,' he babbled, 'oh for sure David would play it and the whole world seemed such a melodic, loving place. He was followed by Asher, and his name means blessed.' He was now quite animated when he added, 'You see we felt blessed by having been given the gift of another perfect child. Lastly there was my lovely, lovely daughter, Dalia, who like her name was indeed a precious flower.' Hans became sad again. 'Dalia, my Dalia was precious and hadn't even celebrated her fourth birthday when...' He was now weeping profusely. 'She lay broken and ... they were all gone, Kate ... all gone.'

He stopped for a full two minutes – two minutes of complete silence except for the tick, tick, ticking of the old granddaughter clock. Eventually Hans managed to mutter, 'All that was so very dear and irreplaceable to me ... in life then ... was no more.'

Another long silence followed before he continued with, 'Do you know that the final blitzkrieg on Warsaw began on the night of 25 September 1939, and it was relentless? Over one thousand of the Luftwaffe planes continually bombed us. There was no place to escape to. We were sitting targets. The Polish airforce had been destroyed in the first week of September ... no blame could be laid on these brave, brave young men. The poor souls tried their very best but they were so heavily outnumbered and their aeroplanes were out-classed by the German ones. The last of my family, my loyal wife, Esther, my sons, David, Asher and my pretty little daughter, Dalia, were murdered on that Sunday night. Only my cousin Josef and I survived and we fled Warsaw on Tuesday 26 September. That was only the day before Warsaw could do nothing other than surrender on Wednesday 27 September 1939.' By the way he was so punctilious in his recall of the dates Kate knew that they were imprinted in his mind forever.

A further strained silence now took over both Hans and Kate. Kate's late father's granddaughter clock loudly tick, tick, ticked the seconds as they passed. Eventually, when Kate could bear the strain no more, she whispered, 'And where does all that you have told me tonight leave us, Hans?'

Leaning over he sought her hand and this time she allowed him to enclose it in his. 'That is what I hope you will tell me. You see, yes, I loved Esther,' he sighed. 'I still do but I adore you just as I adored her. You have been my passport back into wishing to go on living ... before you death was preferable.'

Kate nodded. She accepted what he had just said because to have done otherwise would have broken her heart. She loved him and she knew he was telling the truth because, even though Hans now fully consumed her life, she still loved Hugh. She gave a little sigh as she accepted that there was no way that she could ever forget her first love, her young love, gallant Hugh who at eighteen had made the ultimate sacrifice at Gallipoli.

She was about to ask Hans about the newsreels and other things about his past life when they heard the front door open. Both Kate and Hans then looked towards the inner door and they were surprised when Johnny, Kate's brother, entered.

'Where's Mum?' was Johnny's first desperate question.

Kate, bewildered, looked about the room before uttering, 'I thought she was up at your house with Connie. She said Connie was a bit poorly so she had offered her a hand with Rosebud and Jackie.'

Johnny and Kate stared accusingly at each other before Johnny mumbled, 'Connie says Mum has been acting a wee bit funny of late.'

'Nonsense,' exploded Kate. Turning to Hans she said, 'You don't think Mum has been ... well not herself of late, Hans?'

Hans lowered his head and then appeared to give his feet his full attention. Before raising his head again he rubbed his hands together and then ran his fingers through his hair. Without looking directly at either Kate or Johnny, he began to speak so quietly that both Johnny and Kate had to strain to hear him. 'Well I think your mum, my dear mother-in-law, Jenny, is becoming ... like a lot of old people.'

'In what way?' demanded Kate.

'Look,' he continued, 'I know of a disease that affects old people.' Hans now hesitated because he did not wish to offend Kate and Johnny. 'My grandfather died of it and a woman who also succumbed to these unusual symptoms had her brain tissue examined by a German neurologist, Doctor Alois Alzheimer.'

Johnny, eyes blazing, interrupted, 'Look, Hans, what has all this to do with my mother?'

'Just that for about three months now, your mother has been displaying similar behaviour patterns.'

Johnny turned to Kate. 'Look, I know he is educated but do you think you could get him to get to the point and tell me in plain English what is wrong with Mum?'

Kate looked directly at Hans, and although she chose to say nothing, her eyes pleaded with Hans to do as Johnny had asked.

'Well this Alzheimer doctor examined the brain tissue of a woman who, as I have said, had an unusual mental illness.'

'I trust she was dead when all this took place?' snorted Johnny.

'Of course she had expired and because her symptoms were like your mum's...'

'Kate, when is he going to get to the point?'

Hans ignored Johnny's further outburst and quickly added, 'Which included memory loss, language problems, and unpredictable behaviour.'

Johnny turned to Kate again. 'Well your husband has just listed what I think is wrong with him but that is by the by. Have you noticed any of what he has just described in our mum?'

'To be truthful, Johnny, I have to keep telling her what day of the week it is, the time, the month and she never knows whether she's had a meal or not.'

'Aye, but we all have days like that when we're no sure what's going on,' Johnny blustered.

'But yesterday, Johnny, she thought that the minister, who had called to see if she was all right, was trying as she said to get ... well fresh with her! Mind you he's new and I don't think she likes the way he kisses everybody when he comes to the church door to thank them for coming.'

'Kisses everybody? Surely no the men an all? Oh no, he's no one of them?'

'One of what?' asked Kate.

Johnny was flustered. 'You ken what I mean ... men that dinnae ken ... well ... they just dinnae ken what they want to be.'

'Are you meaning that they are not sure whether to stay Protestant or turn Roman Catholic?'

Coughing to control her embarrassment, Kate spluttered, 'Something like that, Hans, but let's get back to Mum. I mean where do you think she is?'

Johnny shrugged. 'Your guess is as good as mine. Mind you, I hope she has not got in tow with that Jessie Ford who moved into the flat opposite us.'

'Is there something wrong with this Jessie Ford?' asked Hans.

'Well, Hans, she didn't get the name the Blonde Bombshell because she is explosive.'

'Be fair, Johnny, I agree she is as thick as two short planks but her heart's in the right place.'

'You don't agree with Kate?'

'No, Hans, I don't. And it has nothing to do with her being tarry fingered. Plenty of honest folk are that.' Kate giggled because during the war Connie, Johnny's now wife, supplemented the meagre rations by helping herself to all the contraband she could lay her hands on. 'It's just she's a fast bit,'

Johnny continued, whilst running his finger around the inside of his shirt collar. 'I mean Connie told me that last week she asked Mum to go to the pictures with her but it certainly wasn't a James Mason that they saw ... well they couldnae because Fairley's notorious dance hall doesnae show films. Poor Mammy thought that they were there to help the sailor boys write home to their mums. But luckily, the laddies were looking for nubile eighteen-year-olds...'

'So our Mum who is sixty-five wouldn't be in any danger then.' Kate, who was anxious to get the conversation on to how they were going to search for Jenny, butted in.

'Aye you're right there but being evicted because she was giving the place a bad name must have been very...'

'Evicted? They never evicted our mother!'

'They did! You see they have an age limit and from last week, not only do you need to be at least eighteen, but you have to look under forty!'

'That's enough from the two of you,' an irritated Hans announced. 'Now let's go out and look for Jenny.'

'Look for Mum? Oh, Hans, the whole population of Leith and their dogs are out celebrating the end of the war. I mean which crowd would we start with?'

Just then the door opened and in tottered a dishevelled Jenny.

'Oh Mum,' Kate gasped before placing her left hand over her mouth.

Hans went over and escorted Jenny towards a chair. 'Where have you been, Jenny dear?' he asked as he smoothed down her hair.

Lifting her hand Jenny stroked Hans' face. 'Don't know where I've been. But I wanted to get back home and there were so many people, so much noise...'

'Never mind, Jenny. You're home now and you're safe ... so how about a nice cup of tea?'

Johnny had already left for the kitchen and he shouted back, 'I'll make the tea.' Truth was emotion was overpowering him. The last thing he wished was for anyone to see that tears were brimming in his eyes ... actually falling. Looking at his mother in disarray had upset him. After all, his mum who had always been so smart, so well groomed, and oh so proper – Johnny laughed inwardly as he recalled how she wouldn't go out of the house without wearing a hat. 'That is the difference between a woman and a lady,' she would proclaim. 'A woman will tie her hair up in a scarf – a lady always dons a hat.' Johnny's mirth now turned to sorrow. He just didn't know how he was going to cope with watching his mum lose control. Watch day by day as the mother he knew changed.

'Know something, Johnny,' Kate simpered, 'the kettle won't boil if you don't light the gas underneath it.'

Johnny nodded. 'Aye.' But instead of Johnny striking a match he threw his arms around Kate and the both of them swayed backwards and forwards as grief and fear engulfed them.

It was nine-thirty when Kitty and Dotty emerged from the nurses' home. Both were clutching a late-night pass.

'Look out everybody. The night shift has arrived and we are raring to go,' Dotty yelled as she grabbed hold of Kitty's arm and they started to run towards the top of Bangor Road where a very lively party was still in progress.

Kitty stopped abruptly to descend into fits of laughter. There at the top of the Bangor Road, where you could usually find Peggy selling plates of buckies during the day, sat the old Newhaven Fishwife still selling her wares.

'Well if it's not you, Kitty, Sandra's pretty Kitty, then I don't know who it is,' the old Leith landmark chuckled as she filled a saucer of her vinegary doused delicacies and handed it to Kitty. Kitty fished in her purse to pay not only for her saucer of buckies but also Dotty's.

'No. No, lass,' Peggy crooned. 'Sure if I couldnae treat a couple of angels to a plate of buckies I would be in some poor state, so I would. Besides every time I see you I think you are growing more like your mum. Oh, your mammy, now there was a lass who could charm the birds out of the trees.' The old woman grew serious and she leaned over towards Kitty. Kitty knew that Peggy was going to impart something to her that she did not wish the whole world to know so she bent down towards the old woman. 'None of my business, you understand, Kitty.' Kitty nodded. 'But your granny was along here today with that Jessie Ford.'

'Jessie Ford?' queried Kitty.

'Aye, her that got the house that your step-mother, Connie, had to give up when she got pinned on to your dad.'

'Oh, I don't know her ... never met her.'

'Then keep it that way.'

'Why?'

'Well, she frequents Fairley's dance hall up in Leith Street so you'll ken that she is more chased than chaste.' Peggy's lips were now pursed. 'Mind you it's hard to believe that her likes can claim to be a Bowtow. True Bowtow lassies wouldnae sell themselves for a dollar. Wouldnae sell themselves at all, unless they had got tired of living. And here, do you ken that Jessie is also running about with that Edna Stewart?'

'But Edna Stewart is married to my pal Laura's brother. Prisoner of war he is.' Kitty started to chuckle. 'Was. I mean after today all the prisoners will be free and on their way home.'

Peggy shook her head. 'And see when he gets back, I hope the poor laddie gies his Edna a right good doing. And she has asked for it. Honestly, I was talking to his mother, Nessie, and she was saying...' Peggy was now cocking her head knowingly, 'that her Eric will no be hearing from her what Edna's been up to. Mind you with her having a year-old toddler and him having been a prisoner of war since Dunkirk, I don't think any of us will have to say anything. I mean the proof is running about in shitty nappies. But ken this, there is something I would take pleasure in telling him, and that is just what a lazy dirty bitch he got himself hitched to.'

Kitty and Dotty had finished their buckies and Kitty passed the saucers back to Peggy who waggled them 'clean' in a pail of water that had been at her side all day.

The girls said their goodbyes to Peggy and had just started to walk towards a street party that was being held on the Junction Bridge when Dotty drew up and wiped her hand over her mouth. 'Here, Kitty.' She began rhythmically patting her cheeks. 'That pail that Peggy washed the plates in ... well I mean it's a right cesspit is it not?'

'Possible ... but see her and her mother Maggie, who sits on the other side of the street from the crack of dawn until late afternoon, they sit there gutting and selling the fish that their menfolk have caught ... and Leith folk depend on them for cheap, nourishing, wholesome food, and okay the hygiene is not what Matron would tolerate, but to date nobody in Leith has ever died because of it.'

Dotty shrugged. 'Aye, you might be right about the fish but tell me about the fishy tale?'

'Buckies don't have tails.'

'You know fine what I mean. This story about Edna ... I just couldn't believe it. I mean I've been out with Laura and you so often and all she has ever spoken about is her nephew ... you know, the wee lad that's going to school in August ... what's his name? Come on, Kitty, stop playing the fool.'

'I'm not playing the fool, Dotty. Oh Dotty...'

'What?'

'Laura's brother, Eric, well ... you have to know their Mother, Mrs Stewart, who everybody calls Nessie, to understand everything. You see when Edna told Eric she was well...'

'In the family way.'

Kitty nodded. 'And Mrs Stewart, like my granny Jenny would have done, insisted that he marry

Edna. To be truthful most people thought where Edna was concerned that the, "Last Man Freed All" but Eric loved Edna and could see no wrong in her, so they married. He was idle when war broke out so he enlisted. The lad just wanted a steady wage coming in for his wife and his wee newborn son.'

'Is that wee Billy that Laura is always on about?'

Kitty nodded. 'Aye, he mainly stays at Granny Stewart's. To be truthful he thinks Laura is his mother!'

'What?!'

'And what do you think Eric will think of that?'

'Like everybody else he'll probably think that if his mum and Laura had left the bringing up of Billy to Edna she might not have gone off the rails.'

Dotty stopped abruptly and grabbed Kitty's arm and pulled her around to face her. 'Kitty, for heaven's sake ... what I mean is ... stop being your usual diplomatic self and spit out what the story is all about.'

'It's just that when Edna asked Mrs Stewart if she would look after Billy to let her go out and do some war work, well, Mrs Stewart was delighted that Edna wanted to do something to help get the war ended. It wasn't her fault that Edna's idea of servicing the forces wasn't making soup and sandwiches for them.'

'And now Eric will be coming home and there is the wee lassie ... Dotty, sure the bairn is not to blame but most folk, especially Mrs Stewart, won't look at her ... what kind of a life is that bairn going to have?'

51

'Will that not depend on how Eric receives the wee lassie?'

Kitty nodded and smiled. 'Och, you're so right, Dotty. I'm just forgetting how he stood by Edna when wee Billy was on the way. So if he got his arithmetic wrong then he could get it wrong again and things could work out okay.'

'Are you joking?'

'No. You see Eric is a quiet lad. Honestly I have never ever heard him shout. Even when the men in the pub were all going on about Hibs' chances of winning the Scottish Cup, he never lost it. So there's every chance he won't get his running shoes on.'

Dotty pursed her lips and nodded. 'Kitty, know what has just dawned on me? The way you go on about Eric, did you ever have a ... well ... sort of have a fancy for him?'

'Don't be ridiculous, Dotty. I am just coming up twenty years old and I have no intention of getting mixed up with any old man of twenty five.' Dotty's response was to pucker up her face so Kitty was forced to spit, 'And you can pull all the faces you like, Dotty, but get this straight – the very idea of an old man making love to me makes me shudder.'

Dotty's reaction was to laugh out heartily. 'And what about handsome, dashing Doctor Dougal having the hots for you and he must be...?' Dotty stopped and then pretended to work out on her fingers just how old Dougal was.

Irritated by Dotty's actions Kitty was about to rage in retaliation, but when she looked ahead her jaw dropped. There in the State Picture House doorway was Doctor Dougal McNeill, who had begged her, actually begged her, to go to the pictures with him, shamelessly cornering a giggling Audrey Skillon. Although incensed by this spectacle Kitty pretended to mellow and purred, 'Dotty, my dear, why don't you just turn around and you'll see that when Audrey Skillon is about I'm not even in the running.'

'Okay, that might all be true but take my word for it – he does fancy you.' Dotty sighed before forlornly adding, 'But what's the poor guy going to do when he finds out that you wouldn't be able to cope with an old man creeping over you.'

'What on earth are you talking about now?'

Dotty stopped to count on her fingers again before drawling, 'Now correct me if I'm wrong, Kitty, but he must be going on, twenty-six or is it … twenty-seven years old!'

By the time Johnny had pulled himself together and had sat down to talk things over with Kate and Hans, about what they would need to do about Jenny, his beloved dependable mother, an hour had passed. As they went round and round the alternatives it became evident that they could reach no conclusion that suited them all. The main stumbling block was that Johnny wished the problem to be kept from the outside world, thinking they should stand together and protect Jenny. Kate did see his point of view but she felt that they should consult Doctor Hannah, who had known Jenny since he had taken up practice in Leith several years ago. Johnny could see her reasoning but he quietly asked, 'But what if Doctor Hannah thinks that as Mum is not reasoning well...' He gulped before adding, 'Or is losing her mind ... he might have her put away in the...' he gulped again but this time with a shudder before adding, 'the loony bin.'

'Loony bin,' queried Hans. 'What does Johnny mean by loony bin?'

'You have to excuse him, Hans. My dear brother has always had difficulty in remembering when he is at home and not on the shop floor or standing in the sawdust.'

Johnny's face fired. 'Sorry, what I mean is the Royal Edinburgh Hospital in Morningside who deal with people who have ... well they are not...' It was obvious that Johnny was struggling to find words that would not offend Kate again.

Coming to his rescue Kate said, 'Quite as well in their mind as they should be.'

'But surely your mother is just suffering from what that German Doctor Alzheimer has diagnosed.'

'And what exactly is that?' snapped Johnny.

'Just, as I have already said, an old person's condition where they get a bit forgetful. But they can get by ... all they need is a bit of help from their loving families.'

However, before either Kate or Johnny could enquire further of Hans, a rather disorientated Jenny stumbled back into the room.

'Mum,' Kate cried as she skipped over and took her mother into her arms. 'I've just tucked you up in bed ... so why did you get up again?'

Jenny could only shrug. Completely ignoring Kate she looked about the room and from her demeanour it was evident that she was having difficulty recognising everything – putting it all into place in her mind.

It was then Kate decided to guide her mother over to the sofa where she sat her down. Glancing at Johnny, whom she noticed was looking as if he was trying to imitate a gasping fish, she said, 'Johnny, you go and make Mum some tea and I'll sit here with her. Hans, you can make yourself useful by tending to the fire.'

'But it is not cold,' Hans protested, looking over at the open windows.

'You mightn't be shivering but my mum is, so just blooming put a match to the fire, and close the blinking windows.'

Three hours later, when it was well past eleven o'clock, Johnny managed to get himself home. As he had approached his tenement home he had glanced up at his flat and saw that Connie had opened the top windows to allow fresh air to circulate around the house.

Every step that he took as he mounted the stairs was laboured. The day had started out with disappointment in that he had not been nominated as the first choice for the parliamentary seat of his beloved Leith. And by rights, with all the fighting he had done for better working conditions for the workforce, it should have been his, and yet it had been handed to Hoy – and why? – because he was a brainbox – a clever – aye too clever by half boyo. But then, as he hesitated, with his foot on the first step of the final flight to his house, he conceded he had been first choice for the Wider Granton area and that was where most of his workmates were, or would be, housed in the new housing estates there. He had been so buoyed up by Jock when he had pointed out what a chance he had been handed. Then when he had got home to tell Connie – his Connie, who had brought back the sunshine into his life – well – if he did win the election how could he possibly go off to London and leave Connie at forty years of age to cope with three bairns – one not even born yet? He was now at his front door, but before he could fish in his pocket for the key, the door opened and Connie, dressed in a nightgown and smelling of Palmolive soap, stood aside to let him enter.

'Darling, where on earth have you been? I've been so worried. You said you wouldn't be long as you had things to discuss with me.'

Johnny shook his head before slumping down on to his old, worn but very comfy armchair.

'Something amiss, darling?'

Looking from the window Johnny became aware that this was the first night that the blackouts had not had to be pulled over and he smiled when he saw a slight reflection of the moon.

Delaying responding to Connie, he thought about how he had really believed that when the war was at last over it would all be plain sailing in his life. Yet here he was with the dream that he had so wished for – although he told everyone that being a Member of Parliament was not for the likes of him – within his grasp and yet it was now to be so cruelly snatched from him. And not because he wasn't suitable or able – oh no, it was because of his family circumstances. Connie saw him nod as he thought that there would have been a slight chance of his going to London if it was just Connie and the children that he would have to make arrangements for assistance, but his mind was now back to Kate...

Once Kate had quietened their mother down and got her safely tucked back up in bed again she took the opportunity to say to Johnny, 'Look, brother, we have had one of the best mothers in the world, never ever did she let us down. Always there to bolster us up and give us the courage to go on when we just wanted to lie down and lick our wounds, so now, I'm sorry, son, but it's payback time.'

Johnny had nodded his agreement. He then thought back to how his mum had supported Kitty and taken on some of the burden when Sandra had died. How she had thought that he and Sandra had been too young to marry but had made life as easy as she possibly could for them. And when she was vacating the room and kitchen in Ferrier Street she had spoken to the landlord to let him and Sandra take over the tenancy. She had even left the fire still burning in the grate. It had been important to her that they and her grandchildren moved into a warm and welcoming house.

His face was now awash with silent tears but he managed a smile when he recalled that when his mother had cradled hours old motherless Rosebud in her arms his father had said, 'You know son, if your mother could, she would breastfeed the wee lassie for you.' He was still mulling over his mother's condition when he felt a gentle tug on his sleeve. Looking up, he became aware of

Connie speaking to him, but her words and the manner in which she said them made him feel even worse. Oh yes, as he expected now, there stood faithful Connie ... a stalwart of a woman whom he had grown to love. A woman he was so indebted to for taking on the job of mothering his children and running his household. But...

Guilt now swamped him because he knew he should be begging her forgiveness. Forgiveness was necessary because he had deceived Connie by leading her to believe that she had filled the all-consuming, dark, pitiless void that Sandra's premature death had left him with. But in all honesty he now knew that no one could ever mean to him what Sandra had. He did love Connie as much as he could now love anyone but – she was not Sandra. 'Dear God please forgive me,' he begged silently, 'but I just can't love and adore anyone like I worshipped my beautiful Sandra.'

Still keeping his secret to himself he lifted his hand up and placed it over Connie's, which was now resting on his shoulder. 'Sorry, love, you were saying?'

'Just wondering, what's amiss with you? And when you left to visit your mum you said we would have to talk when you got back so why not clear the air between us and let us just ... be honest with each other?'

'Connie, up until tonight I did not think there was anything that could ever happen to my mother. I thought she was indestructible. And now...'

'And now? Look, Johnny, pull yourself together. Your mum is just getting old. After all, she is sixty-five.'

'I know that. That, "Miss Know-all" of a sister of mine told me that half an hour ago and she also had the blasted cheek to say that as life expectancy in Leith right now is fifty-nine we are lucky to have had her for so long.'

Connie started to cackle. 'For heaven's sake ... get a grip, Johnny. Your mum is failing but she's hardly on her way over to Alec Stoddard's to get boxed.'

'I'm not an idiot, Connie. I ken that,' Johnny spat as he roughly brushed Connie's hand from his shoulder. 'But she's my mum and I just dinnae want to see her die slowly day by day. Change from the woman I knew. Don't you realise Connie, she was the woman who could sort out any of my problems and do it without expecting a word of thanks ... my mammy ... my darling Mammy that I could always turn to.' Sobs choking him he then spluttered, 'Can't you see that watching her turn into a dribbling confused stranger, who in the end will not know who I am, will be more than I can bear?'

Connie was now standing behind Johnny and she lifted her hands and began to massage his wracking shoulders. 'There, there, son. I don't want to see it either. But right now she is managing. What she requires is a wee bit of support. And she'll get that because, Johnny, it's payback time for all of us. And if we all work together she can still have a good life and know that we all love her.'

Johnny took out a handkerchief and began to noisily blow his nose. Sniffing he said, 'Of course you and Kate are right. Aye, she said too that we have to look after her. So that means... Connie, remember I said we had things to discuss, well...'

'Well what?'

'Connie, I've been selected to stand for the Wider Granton seat for Labour. They are sure I would get it, but now...'

Connie was now in front of Johnny and she took his face in her hands and as she rubbed his cheeks she said, 'Darling, that's just so wonderful. And just think how proud all the family will be.' She stopped to chuckle before adding, 'Know what, I can just hear your mother standing in the Store butcher's queue saying, "my son's a right honourable now."'

Pressing his hands over Connie's, Johnny sighed before saying, 'That is just it, with Mum the way she is, I can't go.'

'And do you think that Kitty, Kate or I would allow you to give up your dream? See you robbed of what you have worked for ... denied the opportunity to be somebody?'

'It's not only Mum I have to stay for...'

'No?'

He hesitated, and as he took hold of her right hand he muttered, 'There is also you and the fact that I have put you in the family way again.'

'So? Am I some sort of useless, delicate china doll? Don't be daft. Just think of the lassie next door to us now. Same age as me she is and she has had to face her man no coming back from the bloody war and now she's left with seven bairns, and those youngest two laddies of hers ... well they'll certainly no be going to Eton unless they own up to the fact it is just an approved school for posh delinquents!'

Half an hour after Johnny had left, Kate and Hans agreed that as his shop was doing so well, they could afford for Kate to give up full-time work in the Leith Provident store and work as a part-time assistant in Hans' business. This arrangement would allow Kate to be at home with her mother, especially in the mornings when her mother most needed help and guidance.

They were now at the stage of relaxing with a cup of tea when Kate said, 'Thank you, Hans, for making things easy for my mum. Now, before Johnny came in we were talking about what is bothering you. I now know about your family but what we didn't discuss was why you didn't tell me about how you felt about the concentration camps. Did you somehow think I wouldn't understand? Not be as disgusted and moved to pity the way that you are?' Hans could only look down at his feet and continually rub his hands together but reply he did not. 'I am very well aware that awful memories are disturbing you. We both have to accept that they should have been left undisturbed in your subconscious but the newsreels have awakened them. Hans, my dear, they will not go back to sleep again so what I wish you to know is that I am here to help you to cope. Can't you see that if I know what is troubling you I will understand your dilemmas and therefore I will be able to help you to come to terms with it all?'

Hans remained silent but his eyes were brimming with silent tears. Kate went over and knelt in front of him. She then placed her hands on his knees. 'Darling,' she whispered, 'can't you see that if we are to have any sort of future together you have to, and I mean right now, start to think about what you have to do to know peace again?'

Taking her hands into his and looking directly into her eyes he stammered, 'Firstly, now you know how much I loved my wife and children, please tell me that you don't feel threatened?'

Slowly shaking her head Kate lifted her hand to stroke his face. 'No. No, my love. I love you because you are the most loving of human beings that I have ever met. If you had not loved your family, missed them, or deeply regretted what had happened to them how could you be the man that I love? The man I was so glad to marry.' He didn't respond so she tentatively asked, 'You do love me don't you?'

Encircling her tightly in his arms he rocked her backwards and forwards. Hoarsely he whispered, 'Love you? Oh, if it was not for you I wouldn't care whether I live or die. Before I met you I just longed for death to end my suffering. Until you came into my life nothing made my grief bearable.'

She nodded. 'So now what happened today to bring out this desire to tell me what you should have told me years ago?'

'In the newsreel, I am sure it was my cousin Josef that I saw. He seems to be working with the Red Cross in a big house somewhere down in the South of England. Very good people they appear to be, and they are trying to reconnect some of the children who have survived the Holocaust with their relatives.' He paused. 'But for some there will be no one to unite them with ... no one to care for them ... no one to give them a home, love and hope.'

'Are you saying you wish to visit where Josef is and perhaps...'

'If I could, I would wish to adopt them all but I know that if I managed to help one or two of these poor children then I will have done something.' He looked Kate straight in the eye before adding, 'But I...' He halted and as emotion engulfed him his head shook from side to side.

Kate's response was to get up off her knees and place herself on his lap. She then cradled his head in her hands. 'But you are afraid of what I will think ... or wish to do?'

'Yes, you see, it has always been just you and me and we have not had to share our love, or life, or even consider anyone else.' She nodded because she agreed that they had been selfish and had deliberately not allowed anyone into their world – their fairy-tale world – a world that they wished to exclude any contention from.

Hans waited but before Kate had time to reply he said, 'You are over forty. You have never been a mother. Never sat up all night nursing a sick child and I would be asking you to take on a child or children who have been traumatised, so badly damaged by horrors that no human being should endure or witness. Kate, settling those little survivors will be so very difficult.'

Rising she sat herself down in the chair opposite him. Very quietly she said, 'Hans, today is the day for confessions. You say, my dear, that I have never been a mother, never cried for the loss of a child. Oh, if only that was true.' Still keeping her distance from him she poured out the story of the love she had had for Hugh. In graphic detail she described Hugh as he was to her then and still was to her today. With pride she told of how he was a tall, dashing, handsome lad whom she had loved so very much and still did – that was why she understood that Hans still loved his first wife and yet could also intensely love her too.

It was very difficult for Kate to go on and say that she had allowed Hugh to make wonderful physical love to her all night long. This act in 1915 was judged to be a disgraceful, lustful sin, and if it was, she was glad to have been a transgressor. She then went on to confess to Hans that never once in her whole life had she regretted that wonderful night – not even now. All that was left to tell Hans was that the reckless night of passion had resulted in Hugh accidentally leaving her, a vulnerable naive fifteen-year-old, pregnant. Unaware of her situation he had then gone off to fight and die in the First World War. Kate was now softly crying as she haltingly told Hans through wracking whimpers how she had fallen down some stairs and miscarried her baby.

The natural question for Hans to ask was if she had had any other lovers since Hugh, but he knew without being stupid enough to put such a crass question what the answer was.

Kate looked over to him and she was moved by the compassion she saw his eyes. 'So, my darling,' she murmured, 'if you are saying that you wish to go and seek out Josef so you can adopt a child then I am more than willing to become some-one's mother.'

'But how could we? There is the shop and now there is also ... your mother.'

'Well it is now May so it will soon be the first week in July and that is the week we have the Edinburgh trades holiday week. That means we can shut up the shop for at least seven days. And don't worry about my mum. Connie will look after her whilst we are away. Taking on my share of the caring as well as her own will be no problem to Connie.'

Hans was now standing and he pulled Kate up on to her feet but then a frown passed over his face. 'That all sounds very well but have you forgotten that your brother may be fighting an election in July?'

Kate gasped. 'Oh, Hans, I was so taken up with you and my mum that I forgot to ask Johnny how the selection meeting went. Blast!'

The Taylor Gardens street party for the end of the war was still in full swing when Laura, accompanied by the new love of her life, Mike Bailey, bumped into Kitty, Dotty and the staff from Leith Hospital, who were enjoying the revelry.

When Kitty espied Laura she waved her arms wildly in the air and hollered, 'Laura, Laura, it's just great to see you.'

The two young women embraced before they began to dance around the street. 'Oh, Kitty, isn't it just wonderful that it's all over. My mum who, as you know, never shows any emotion, just burst into tears and wiped them away on the bottom of her apron.'

'No wonder, Laura. She will be so relieved that

at last Eric, her quiet, docile laddie, who wouldn't say boo to a mouse, will soon be on his way home from that hellish prisoner-of-war camp.'

'I know that. And I do truly believe what my Granny says, and that is that our Eric is, "one of nature's gentlemen" so the imprisonment won't have changed him ... but Kitty, I can't but worry that being a prisoner of war *may* have changed him.'

'We've all changed in five years, Laura. That's how life is.'

'But Kitty, what if my soft big brother is very different from what he was? What then?'

'Och, Laura, as I've already said, since the blooming war started we've all had to grow up, mature, accept the blows.' The hardest blow for Kitty in the war had been the loss of her brother, Jack. Losing him had been so hard to bear – even tonight she felt the need to cry for him – mourn for him. But pulling herself together she thought, no, tonight is a night for celebrating, so she grabbed Laura again and whispered, 'But no matter what, Laura, underneath there are still parts of the old "us" there.' Stroking Laura's back she added, 'Believe me, parts of us can never be changed. Our childhood made us the adults we are. And, I just know the bairns we were when we ran about the streets playing, and the values we were taught then, still live within us. Look...' Both girls' eyes were now drawn to the crowds who seemed to have lost all their inhibitions. Mature women who always made sure that their skirts were so long that their knees hadn't been seen for years were now kicking their height in gay abandon and it appeared that it didn't matter who saw the tops of their stockings.

Kitty and Laura then convulsed with laughter when old, drunken Sam insisted that Jean Irvine, the old maid schoolteacher, should take a swig from his screw-top beer bottle. Laura then managed to mumble through her giggles, 'Aye, maybe you're right and when my brother gets back he will still be his same old "roll with the punches", just like Jean Irvine is doing now.'

Looking at Laura again Kitty thought that she wasn't really enjoying the celebrations. 'Look Laura, if your long face is because you are worrying about what your Eric will make of Edna's shenanigans, just forget it. He's besotted with Edna. Honestly, if she asked him to lie down so she could walk on top of him he would. And as to the bairn ... I'm sure he will soon be daft about her too.'

A voice saying, 'Here, Laura, have you forgotten that you came to this party with me?' put an end to the girls' chat.

'No. No,' Laura replied. 'Kitty, meet Michael or, as I call him, Tricky Mike.' Kitty nodded and smiled at Mike. She couldn't help but notice that there was something so engaging about him. He was only about five feet ten in height but as he walked with such a nonchalant, aristocratic way he seemed much taller. However, it was not his height that was his main attraction, it was his engaging smile and as he looked at Laura, somehow Kitty knew that he would be the love of Laura's life. She was just so thrilled for them both that she linked arms with them and without a word passing between them they proceeded to do a palais glide along the road. The scene was so happy and magical that looking at those young people you could see, with the evil of war laid to rest, that the future should be so much easier for them. By the very way they were cavorting around Taylor Gardens, you could see they were the future of the country and they would make a good stab at making it a better place for their future children.

It was well past midnight when Kitty and Dotty arrived at the door to Leith Hospital nurses' home and they were surprised that the door was opened for them by the night sister who gleefully asked, 'I do so hope you have had a good time tonight.' She looked beyond them towards Doctor Dougal McNeill, and her voice chilled when she said, 'Doctor you look to me to be well under the influence of Al.Co.Hol and I would therefore suggest you get yourself to wherever your bed is, and it is certainly not in this block!' She then turned her attention to Kitty and Dotty again. 'Ladies,' she began her tone now professional, 'that young man is trouble. Take my advice and steer clear of him.'

Dotty looked at Kitty and she was about to say that she agreed with the night sister but there was something about the way Kitty was looking at Dougal that had her think that far from shunning Dougal, Kitty might gladly submit to his charms.

# PART TWO

## EARLY JUNE 1945

Hans had just finished turning the keys in the double locks of his shop door when Maryann called out to him, 'Aye, that's lucky you finishing up for the day and poor wee me just starting.'

Turning to greet Maryann, Hans smiled. 'Aye, I did intend to be all locked up by twelve thirty so I could get back to Kate but two couples came in to buy engagement rings.' Unconsciously Hans started to rub his hands together. 'Just as well I got new stock in yesterday.'

'Aye, right enough I was wondering why the postie needed a signature from you yesterday.' She chuckled. 'I just knew, you being you and not a penny going the wrong way, and your Kate so against the "never never", it just couldnae hae been a bad debt letter.'

Hans laughed. 'No, no. See since the men started coming home I just can't keep up with them all wanting to buy engagement rings, wedding rings and nice small gold watches.'

'Right enough and it's a pity you dinnae sell prams because by this time next year there will be so many bairns being born we'll run out of nappies.'

By now Maryann was mounting the stairs to the Palace Picture House back door but she drew up abruptly and placed her hand over her mouth as blood rushed to her face. 'Oh, Hans, forgive me for being so flippant. I mean ... with Jenny just being buried yesterday I should have been asking how Kate and her brother were coping. And I know Alex Stoddard would have given Jenny a nice send-off. Bet he boxed her up in polished mahogany with shining brass handles.' Hans did not reply so Maryann added, 'Always gives Leith folk he kens a good send-off, so he does. And with him looking like a corpse himself you are assured of sympathetic support.'

Hans had now drawn away from his shop door and he just stared at Maryann in bewilderment. It was true that Jenny's sudden death had been a shock for the family but both Kate and Johnny, although devastated to lose their mother, were relieved she had died of a heart attack. Their mother going through to the end of dementia would have been just so cruel for her and unbearable for them to witness.

'Mind you, Hans, with your business booming you'll no be wondering where the wherewithal will be coming from to pay for the funeral.'

Amazed that Maryann had the audacity to be speaking about Jenny's private business and her not cold in her grave yet, Hans quipped, 'There will be no need for anyone to pay for anything concerning Jenny. My dear departed mother-in-law had one-penny and two-penny fully paid up policies that will more than cover any expenditure. And if it is any of your business, which it is not, she also left Kate and Johnny a biscuit tin each.'

'A biscuit tin each?' exclaimed Maryann. 'And

what would they be wanting with an old biscuit tin?'

'Oh they won't keep them. They're not old school so they will be depositing them in the bank.'

Maryann started to chuckle. 'Och, Hans, I ken fine that you're from Poland but you've been here long enough to ken that banks in Scotland, especially that one at the top of Bonnington Road that Jenny used, dinnae take old biscuit tins.'

'Oh but they will be wanting those ones and they will also be happy to receive the five little home-savings banks that Jenny put a sixpence into each week for her grandchildren.'

'Are you saying that every week she put a tanner into five of they wee home-savings banks that only the bank can open?'

Hans nodded.

'But for why?'

'Obviously she wanted to leave something for her five grandchildren. And before you ask, what will be happening to Jack's, his one is going to baby Jackie since he was killed recently and she made a surprise arrival just after that.' Before Hans moved off in the direction of Morton Street he cocked his head and gave dumbfounded Maryann a sly wink.

He had just crossed over from Wellington Place and on to the grassy Links itself when he regretted having been so short and rude to Maryann. She had been a very good friend to him and she had tried to assist him whenever she could. He knew for a fact that if anyone mentioned to her that they were thinking of buying jewellery, watches or clocks she always recommended that they purchased from him. He also knew that she was a lonely woman and because he was one of the people she met up with on most days she liked being friendly with him and keeping him up to date with the local gossip. Today he had been unnecessarily rude to her and this was because he was still feeling the loss of Jenny.

Pulling up his coat collar to keep out the unseasonably cold wind, he thought, even the June weather, when you would expect sunshine and warmth, seemed to be mourning Jenny. He then started to rub his hands together – it was as if he was trying to lose the chill that had invaded him in the cemetery yesterday. Vividly he remembered how his Kate, who had insisted on going with her mother on her last journey, had never had a dry face all day. Yes, Kate's tears had mingled with the rain that never stopped flowing.

As he strolled through the Links, Hans began to wonder if Jenny's passing would have any effect on Kate and his cherished plans to go south. He smiled as he remembered how he and Kate had worked out all the arrangements. Connie, although pregnant again, had insisted that Jenny stay with her for the six days that they would be away. The only member of the family who had not been exactly ecstatic about their trip was Johnny.

'Aye,' he had spat through pursed lips, 'you being away from 30 June to 6 July will be just dandy.'

'Dandy?' queried Kate.

'That's right ... dandy because that means that you'll not be here to cast your vote. Or have you forgotten that Thursday the 5th July is polling day? Not that you'll be voting in the seat that I'm fighting but I would have thought you would have stayed faithful to our dad and been here to cast your vote. And just listen to that noise ... that's our suffragette auld granny whirling in her grave now she's discovered that you're not interested in casting your vote in the most important election of our lives.'

Kate's lip was trembling but Johnny was not in a mood to go soft on her so he viciously added, 'Kate, for heaven's sake, don't you realise for us to get the social change we are all crying out for, Labour has to win? That means all our supporters have to get to the ballot box.'

Kate, mouth agape, looked at Hans – who was also looking definitely contrite. Connie, on the other hand, was giving Johnny such hostile looks that had they been darts his face would have looked like a pin cushion.

'Johnny,' she began, 'I think you are forgetting about all the help that Hans and Kate have given you with your campaign. Hans' shop windows are covered in your and Jimmy Hoy's posters. Kate has been out every day for three weeks now knocking on doors. Hans even borrowed his friend Bill Brown's car so he could go out and join her after he had closed up the shop.'

Johnny looked sheepish and everyone was astounded when he asked, 'And talking of Bill, how is he?'

'Red hot, I expect,' countered Connie, 'or is your brain so taken up with getting elected that you have forgotten he was cremated last Friday at

Seafield Crematorium!'

Gulping, Johnny whispered, 'Right enough. He died ... but I got to his service.'

'Aye, but just. Black affronted I was when you burst in the back doors just in time for the final hymn. And in case you've forgotten it was "Abide With Me" which we are all finding hard to do with you right now. Honestly Johnny, you can think of nothing but this blooming election, so much so I hope you win because I could do with you being hundreds of miles away in London all week and me just having to listen to your mantras at the weekend.'

'Look, could we all just cool it and try to find a way around things? Granny gets so upset when the family are at odds with each other,' implored Kitty, who had been listening in to the conversation.

'You're right, Kitty,' Kate replied before looking directly at Hans and suggesting, 'Would us going a week later be so much of a problem?'

Hans shrugged.

'You see, my dear, we could leave late on the Saturday ... now that would be the seventh and return on Friday the thirteenth...'

'But would you wish to be travelling all that way on Friday the thirteenth?' Connie gulped. 'You know how unlucky it's supposed to be.'

Kate shook her head. She wondered if she would ever get used to Connie being so superstitious but wasn't it also like Connie to be thinking of what was best for all family members?

Hans was now nodding. 'Of course, if we leave after closing time on Saturday and be back for opening time the next Saturday we will not lose too much business. So that is what we will do.'

'But the trains are very busy on a Saturday so you are probably too late to book a sleeper now.'

Hans nodded again. 'That's right, Kitty, but I am thinking that I will be asking Bill's widow, I mean Madge, if I could borrow his car for the weekend. That would mean that Kate would be able to sleep on the journey down ... she needs more sleep than I do.'

'But do you think Madge will be okay with that?' Kitty queried.

'Oh, yes, you see she does not drive and she was saying to me that she thinks she would like to just get rid of the car ... just sell it.'

'That makes sense because with Bill gone she won't be having a regular income coming in,' Johnny chorused, feeling great now that he had got his way and all his family would be standing with him – assisting him from now on and up to polling day.

Hans was now thinking that was all arranged then, but Jenny's passing could change everything. He was at his front door when he wondered how he could diplomatically approach Kate, just a day after her mother had been buried, to ask if the sad happening would make any difference to their plans.


Kitty tightened up her silk scarf in an effort to keep out the chill wind that was blowing in the cemetery. It had been her intention to lay the bunch of pink roses that she had bought in Dick's the florist in Great Junction Street on her grandmother's grave, but this would not be possible because two of the gravediggers were still filling in the plot.

One of the cemetery's attendants then stood up to mop his brow with his red polka-dot handkerchief and as the man lowered his hand he exclaimed, 'Well if it's not yourself. And I'm pleased to say I havnae seen you about these parts for a while now. Bet you're back to talk to your mammy again ... hope it's good news this time?'

Kitty shook her head and the water from her soaking hair sprayed over the man but he seemed not to notice. 'No, I haven't come to talk to Mum, well actually I will before I go, you see I just popped in to put these roses on my granny's grave but as she was only buried yesterday you haven't finished filling it in.'

'This auld buddy your granny? Shame it was. Now dinnae ken if you know it but every week she would come in here on a Friday. Sit down on that bench there that looks on to her man's grave, where she is now, and have a wee chat with him. Loved him so she did. And we loved her coming because she always had a couple of newly-baked scones in her bag. Now no for your grandad but for me and Dod there. We'll sure miss her. Great wee baker she was. Missed her vocation, she should have run a bakery.'

Kitty smiled.

'See last Friday, Dod and me we kent that there was something wrang. She sat down right enough to talk to your grandad but she didnae have her message bag with her so we kent there would be nae scones for us. Next thing she starts to quiver

76

and shiver and she looked at us but we kent she wasnae seeing us. I ran to the supervisor's house...' the man now pointed to the caretaker's house in the grounds, 'and got Elsie to make your granny a cup of tea but when I got back with the tea your granny was slumped on top of Dod and I could see that she wasnae breathing any more. Got an ambulance but they could do nothing. Poor soul, I dinnae ken what took her. Mind you I bet her old man was there to take her hand.'

'It was a heart attack. And what I am pleased about, and I am sure you are too, is that it wasn't too painful.'

'It wasn't?'

'No. You see because she was so old and her heart wasn't in good shape ... it was quick. Good for her but...' Kitty started to cry and sodden as the bench was she dropped down on it. The grave-digger sat down beside her and very tenderly he wiped her tears away. 'I would just so have liked to have said goodbye to her. Thank her for being the best granny in the world.'

'Now,' the gravedigger said forcibly, 'don't you worry yourself about that. See it's our job to keep the graves nice and tidy and after I heard you talking to your mammy I thought that whilst I'm working about she would like a word or two from me an all. Oh aye, your mammy kens the war's ower and it will be no problem to keep your granny up to date tae.'

Instead of these comforting words consoling Kitty she howled even louder and the gravedigger was relieved when Laura came into the cemetery and took over comforting Kitty from him.

On leaving the cemetery the two girls strolled, arm in arm, over the Links and then got themselves seated at a table for two in Smith's Tearooms on the corner of Morton Street.

The pot of tea for two and two fruit scones had just been deposited on the table and Kitty and Laura started to butter their scones. 'You know,' Laura blurted as she dolloped a spoonful of jam on to her delicacy, 'Kitty, I just want to say how terribly sorry I am that I didn't get to your Granny's funeral yesterday. We have been pals since schooldays and I knew I should be there to support you ... but, oh Kitty...'

This admission by Laura caught Kitty off balance and as she bit into her scone she managed to smear some of the jam over her face. Hastily fishing for a handkerchief from her pocket she firstly wiped the jam off her lips and then she dabbed her eyes that had welled with so many tears that they were cascading down her cheeks.

'Oh Kitty, I didn't mean to upset you,' Laura blubbered, 'it was just that I wanted you to know that I ... look I was ready to come over to your house when all hell broke out at mine.'

Leaning over, Kitty put her hand over Laura's. 'Look, Laura, I'm not going to lie to you and pretend that I didn't know that Eric arrived home three days ago and...'

Laura's tears were now splashing. 'Kitty, he looks so pathetic. You know how he was a sturdy lad ... a bruiser really ... well now he looks like some Belsen horror. Starved he has been and he's ... even quieter. You know how he wouldn't really argue about anything ... well, except Hibs and

Hearts ... but even football doesn't interest him now.'

'He's staying at your mum's?'

Laura nodded. 'When Eric's train got into the Waverley he was in such a hurry to get to his Edna and wee Billy that he took a taxi down to his home in Primrose Street. He told my mum that when he opened the door and threw in his hat, instead of Edna being there to catch it, it was her mum.'

'Her mum? Are you saying it was Judy Fox who was in the house?'

'Aye, Edna was out ... well ... she was out. But even although it was past ten o'clock, wee Billy was still up on the floor so Eric made a grab to cuddle the bairn into him.' Laura paused to catch her breath. 'But the wee laddie, and it wasn't his fault because Eric had been gone five years, didn't know who he was and he got such a fright that he started to bawl. His yelling woke up wee Ella and didn't Eric then ask Mrs Fox whose bairn Ella was and didn't she, because her head is befuddled with the booze, tell him it was Edna's.'

'What happened then?'

'Eric left his kitbag and everything and dashed out of the house and never stopped running until he got to my mum's house. My mum wasn't being disloyal when she told him the truth about Edna. She then got her coat on and she went down to Primrose Street and gathered up all wee Billy's things and the bairn is now living with us.'

'Och, Laura, your mum doesn't deserve all this worry and upset and neither does Eric. But give it a day or two and it might all settle down. I mean that wee Ella is such a darling wee lassie I could adopt her myself.'

'Aye, she is a nice bairn but, oh Kitty, I really do wish that she'd never been born. I wish my poor brother's heart hadn't needed to be broken.'

A long pause fell between the girls and as Kitty lazily stirred her tea Laura could see that her thoughts were far away. Eventually Laura reached over and stroked Kitty's face. 'Penny for them.'

'Just thinking about my granny. Such a shame that she won't be here to see my dad win, and keep your fingers crossed that he doesn't lose the election. She was so proud of him. You see Aunty Kate always seemed to be the one that got on ... she was a manager ... she never put a foot wrong. Helped my granny buy their own house and my dad well he worked in the shipyards and he likes nothing better than to stand with his feet in the sawdust and down a pint,' she giggled, 'or two or three with the boys. And here talking of my granny being thrifty look at this.' Kitty fished in her handbag and brought out the small savings bank that her granny had left for her. 'She left me this.'

'How much is in it?'

Kitty shrugged. 'Don't know. And I don't care. But what I am going to do is keep putting a wee something in it every pay day.'

'Talking of pay day, how about we cheer ourselves up and get ourselves up the Palais on Friday? A night boogieing our blues away is what we need.'

'Would love nothing better and I could do it because my granny didn't believe in this mourning for weeks, never mind months, but as luck would have it I'm on night duty for the rest of the week.'

'Which ward?'

'Accident and emergency would you believe. That means we will be kept busy with all the old drunks that have fallen over, the young men who are back from the war and after a couple of pints, they think they are still fighting it.' Laura laughed. 'You can laugh. But see now the nights are light, most of the wee laddies will be playing at "commando training" in Couper Street's half demolished buildings.' Kitty sighed. 'Then the nursing staff will be run off their feet bandaging their grazed knees and sorting out their broken bones.'

The late Friday afternoon sun had at last some heat in it. Kitty was feeling very fatigued after having been drummed into doing two hours service in her Father's campaign office. As it was important to her that she was very alert for her night-duty stint she decided to go and have a two-hour nap in her room in the nurses' home. However, as she turned her face up to be kissed by the warming rays of the sun, she decided that before going for her nap she would just while away a few minutes sitting on a bench in Taylor Gardens. As she breathed in deeply she noted that she was not the only one appreciating the long-awaited change in the weather – the roses in the hospital gardens were all lazily wafting their perfume into the air.

A voice asking, 'Is this all you've got to do with your time?' had Kitty sitting bolt upright.

'Oh, it's you, Dougal. And isn't this a first for

you ... not one deluded young lassie hanging on your every lying word.'

'Do you know, Kitty, if you would just say that you and I could start courting I would break all my other admirers' hearts and tell them I am strictly a one-woman man now.'

Kitty giggled and clapped her hands. 'Dougal,' she exclaimed, 'you and I both know that your promise to be faithful to me wouldn't last any longer than...' Just then a sassy young lassie skipped by them and as she tottered on her high-heeled shoes she winked at Dougal. He returned her compliment with a licentious smile and Kitty quipped, 'See what I mean?'

'Ah,' he replied, sliding himself nearer to her on the bench, 'but it would be if you would just utter the words I am begging to hear you say.'

Kitty was now as far along the bench as she could be and as she struggled to stand up he jumped up and got down on his bended knees and implored, 'Kitty, pretty Kitty, put me out of my agony and just say that you will be mine.'

Kitty glanced up at the Leith Provident store clock and noted it was now five past five. 'Sorry, Dougal, can't stay. I need to get some beauty sleep. I am on night duty tonight.'

Dougal started to dance around Kitty. 'So am I,' he enthused, 'so why don't we cuddle up together for a couple of hours. I promise you that you will remember these wonderful hours for the rest of your life.'

'Dougal,' an exasperated Kitty hissed, 'have you ever had a psychiatric assessment?'

'No, because I don't need one.'

'That's a matter of opinion because I personally think that the inmates in Bangour mental hospital are saner than you!'

The day after her mother's funeral Kate decided that she was going to be completely in control and businesslike. She knew that her mother had consulted Mr Paterson, an elder in South Leith Parish Church who was also a partner in Sheils and McIntosh the solicitors in Charlotte Street, and that he had drawn up a will for her. So the first thing she had to do was find the will. That was fine until she entered her mother's bedroom and she could still smell her mother.

This exclusive odour that had always wafted from Jenny was a mixture of Yardley's lavender soap that Jenny only used to wash her face – this was because according to her it was too expensive to wash your feet with – and their talc. Birthday and Christmas presents from her dad to her mother were always the same – bar of lavender soap for her birthday and a tin of talcum powder at Christmas. After her father had died Kate had kept up the tradition and there on the dressing table sat two tins of talc and one unused bar of soap. Emotion was now rising within her and she was glad to be alone in the house because wanted to cry and shout and beg for her mother to still be with her. Ten minutes later she opened the middle drawer of the dresser and there, neatly tied with a blue cord, were all the papers that she would need today. Insurance policies, which she knew were there because Jenny was forever telling her that they were, and also the will.

The small banks for the grandchildren that had stood on the mantelpiece in the living room had been handed out to them yesterday. So all that was left today was the will. Kate already knew it was about the disposal of the house – this home, her home, her parents' home that they loved and found such happiness in. She knew she should not open the will until Johnny was with her but she had helped her mum and dad to buy it. It was also true that her mum and dad were fair to both of their children so it was possible that – no – she must not think that. But she had to know. So going over to her parents' bed she sat down. She wanted to take the will from its envelope and learn – just know for sure – what it said – and whatever it said she knew that it would be binding. Running the fingers of her left hand over the satin of the eiderdown that had always kept her mum and dad snug, she silently pleaded, 'Mum, please forgive me but I just have to read your will and find out if Hans and I are going to be– Mum we had such plans.'

Another five agonising minutes passed before she could read what was to be.

Tears, sobs and sighs filled the room. She was not in the clear. By no means was she that. But her mother, fair to the end, had left her a way out. She was to receive one third of the value of the house, at the time of her mother's death. This was because she had contributed to the buying of the house and had always lived there. The remainder, after all legal fees were paid, was to be divided equally between herself and Johnny. Kate had feared, as happened so often and was legal, that the eldest son would get everything. She gave a short tearful giggle but then her mother at heart was what they were now calling not suffragettes but feminists, and she thought it so wrong that one child should be favoured in a will because they were the eldest son.

Kate accepted that her mother's will meant that Hans and herself would be required to buy Johnny out and as soon as possible at that. This was because Johnny lived in a rented house and he had four living children and another on the way. His wife did not work and therefore it would be so wrong of Kate and Hans to expect him to wait for too long for his inheritance. The problem here was Kate had given up her well-paid job in Leith Provident department store. It was true that Hans' business was growing but it couldn't provide a wage like she had had. Besides, she wanted to assist Hans in his desire to help some of the refugee children – she sighed – it was all too much to think about right now. She needed time. She wasn't sure if she would ever be ready to think about it all. She looked up at the bedroom window that had to have the mandatory net curtain that kept anyone from looking in. She smiled because the sun was just ignoring her mother's modesty and was shining brightly into the room. This lovely room that was always so happy, bright and fresh.

Getting up she decided she had to move on so what should she do first? Now what was more obvious than getting herself out for a walk? Whilst she was doing that she would take the old biscuit tin that her Mum had left her and deposit the contents in the bank.

Just as Kate was about to get herself into the bank didn't she discover her darling niece Jackie sitting in her go-car and who should be left to look after her but Rosebud?

'Well hello,' a smiling Kate said to the children. 'Is Mum in the bank?'

'Yes,' replied Rosebud. 'We're skint again so she took an old tin Granny left her in there and she says she is sure that there will be enough in it to get me some new shoes and something really nice for Daddy's tea.'

Kate was a bit taken aback with what Rosebud had said. She had never given a thought as to how Johnny and Connie were managing since his accident. It was true he had a job with the union but it would not be paying much, and certainly with all the overtime Johnny did in the shipyards, not as much as Robbs would have paid him. Wincing, Kate thought again that she and Hans had just thought of themselves.

Before she could really start beating into herself again Connie literally danced out of the bank doors.

'Get a nice surprise, did you?'

'Oh, Kate,' Connie replied whilst rubbing her hands over her purse, 'see your Mum, och, she was a star, was she not? And all mums should be like her. Always helping her bairns she was, even her adult ones, when the feet got kicked from us.' Connie huffed, sighed and smiled before adding, 'Oh, would you believe that just when things have got so bad that Johnny and I were about down on our knees your mum left us a lifeline ... no really a lifeline, more a whaling rope.'

'Things that bad?'

'Aye, you see we were managing to just limp along, and your mother, well God bless her, never came in without a full shopping bag. But with Johnny having to spend a wee, no a big, lump of our earnings on this election thing and your mum sort of ... well, Kate ... no her fault but she just sort of forgot the shopping bag ... life is and was awful.' Connie stopped to hunch her shoulders and give a wee squeal before gleefully muttering, 'But right now I can get next door into Baird's shoe shop and get Rosebud some new shoes. Look at what the wee soul is wearing.'

Kate looked down at Rosebud's feet and where she would have expected to see her clad in Clarks brown summer sandals, the child was wearing last year's scruffy white plimsolls. And if that was not bad enough, the toes had been cut out because they were obviously too small for her.

Before Kate and Connie could continue their conversation Rosebud squealed, 'Mummy, Mummy, are you saying I'm getting new shoes today?' The child then tugged at Kate's skirt before she added, 'Aunty Kate, I'll be getting new shoes today because...' Rosebud drew in a large breath before shouting, 'I've stopped swearing on a Sunday because that's a holy day.'

'That right,' exclaimed Kate looking to Connie for confirmation.

Connie nodded. However, before she could say anything, Rosebud quickly butted in with, 'And on the other days, Aunty Kate, I only say bloody or damn.' She now looked hopefully up at Connie. 'And I haven't said shite since ... since ...

since ... a ... long ... long ... time ago.'

Both Kate and Connie had to purse their lips to keep their laughter in check. Eventually, Connie managed to splutter, 'Look, Kate, you get into the bank and get your nice surprise. And I'll get Rosebud some summer sandals then we can meet round the corner in the café and have a cup of tea ... after all, thanks to your mum we can afford to treat ourselves.'

Kate nodded. There was just something so nice about her sister-in-law. And today Kate was even more aware of this when she had heard Rosebud, whose mother had died giving birth to her, now calling Connie 'Mummy'. A true kind of mother was something that had been missing from Rosebud's life. Adults had surrounded her but no one had given her the love, time and care that Connie had. Kitty, her sister, had just been fifteen when she had had to take on Rosebud and she had done so very well. However, Kate now realised, with the passing of her own mother which had left her devastated, no one in the family had accepted that Kitty had done her best with Rosebud. But how could she really have provided the emotional needs the child required when her heart had been so suddenly and cruelly broken?

Fifteen minutes later Rosebud was parading up and down the café showing off her new shoes to anyone who would look at them. Kate had just lifted the teapot to pour out a cup for Connie and herself when Connie said, 'And how did you feel when they told you how much was in your biscuit tin?'

Kate shook her head and laughed. 'You know I

was so flabbergasted when they told me just how much mum had saved up for me, I nearly dropped. You know I think the old miser must have been blackmailing someone. I did realise that after we bought the house she was so used to putting so much by every week she continued to do that, but with my dad dying and his wages going with him, well, Connie ... see when they told me that there was fifty-four pounds in the box, nearly fainted I did. Asked for a recount ... but it came to the same total.' Leaning over to quietly confide in Connie she said, 'Here, do you think she really was blackmailing someone?'

Connie lowered her head and she seemed relieved when Rosebud asked when her ice-cream cone would be coming. Lifting her head Connie signalled to the shopkeeper to bring two ice-cream cones drenched in raspberry sauce.

Aware that something had upset Connie, and thinking she may have become upset because Kate had suggested that perhaps Jenny had been a blackmailer, Kate changed the subject by saying, 'Mind you, Connie, if Johnny does get elected you will have a decent wage coming in again.'

Connie nodded. The change of subject seemed to brighten her and she bent over and patted Kate's hand. 'You're right there. It's nine hundred a year and one of the first things that the new parliament is going to do is put it up to a thousand, that's a whole grand, Kate.'

To working-class people like Kate and Johnny's family, this wage was a fortune. Kate, of course, being financially aware, replied, 'That's great. I am so pleased for you. You both deserve it. Mind you he will have train fares and other expenses.'

'No. If he gets in, he gets a free rail pass and his stationery and postages paid. There will just be his lodgings from Monday night to Thursday night to come out of his pay.'

'If all that you say is right, Connie, then from today on we all have to get out there and shout from the rooftops that he is the one people should vote for.'

'Aye, things are looking up, Kate, and now with me managing to get Rosebud to stop swearing, she might be allowed to stay in Hermitage Park School in August instead of being evicted by Miss Cameron or Miss Roy.'

Friday the 22nd June 1945, saw Kitty's evening shift begin as was normal now. The usual drunks who had managed to break some bones when they tripped over and argued with the pavements. Women whose husbands thought they were the weekly punchbags. Children who saw themselves as the *Lone Ranger* only to find out that the wall they were riding on wasn't a prancing horse and when they fell off they hit the solid causey stones and split foreheads, grazed knees and fractured arms, all of which had to be attended to at the hospital.

By eleven o'clock things had started to calm down and Kitty was just about to go for her break when Sister Brown called her over. 'Anderson,' she began as she consulted her watch, 'I would like you to get yourself into theatre then get scrubbed up and gowned.'

'I was just...' Kitty began to lightly protest.

'Yes, I know, take your break, but that will have to wait. And you're not the only one to be inconvenienced. Mr Lawson, who should have been home two hours ago, is also having to hang on.'

'Why?'

'We have a serious stabbing case coming in.'

'Sister, that's the ambulance just pulling up,' the night duty porter called out as he bounded up the outpatient department steps.

'Right, everyone to their stations,' Sister commanded.

By the time Kitty had scrubbed and gowned up, the two ambulance men had stretchered in the victim and between them and the theatre staff the young woman was laid out on the operating table.

'Sorry, Mr Lawson,' the senior ambulance attendant began, 'I knew she was dead, or dying, when we got to her ... that the spurting and the great loss of blood meant her carotid artery has been severed. But you see she's so young and well ... I'm told you can do so much nowadays that I thought if we got her to you right away ... well you just might ... save her like you've saved others.'

Mr Lawson looked down at the young woman, who quite obviously had very quickly bled to death and he sighed. Nonetheless, before he announced there was nothing he could do that was going to bring back life into the woman, he examined her wound, felt her pulse and then just raised his hands to signal that life was extinct and that he could not reverse it.

Kitty by now was staring down at the horrific scene and as she backed away from the table she mumbled, 'Who on earth did this?'

'Her man,' was the ambulance man's answer.

'No. No, please God no ... not her husband?' she then screamed.

'Oh, but aye. And the police have arrested him,' the ambulance attendant was pleased to inform them. He then looked reverently at the sister before adding, 'And after they take him into Leith Police Station they'll be coming here to see what he is to be charged with.'

Now completely out of control Kitty lunged towards Mr Lawson. 'Look,' she screamed beating his chest, 'you must try again to bring her back. Please, please. You just have to.'

'Anderson,' Sister exclaimed, 'pull yourself together. I accept that you have probably not attended such a horrific case before but losing your control contributes nothing. We must at all times keep our professionalism. If we don't, further problems could be caused.'

Sobbing Kitty grabbed the sister's arm. 'Please. Try and understand,' she incoherently babbled, 'it's not that I am not moved by Edna Stewart lying there lifeless it's... Oh no, if it's ... and please God don't let it be true that it was her husband Eric, that ... oh no Laura, her mum, wee Billy. You see Eric ... he has just come home from being kept a prisoner and now...'

'Anderson, who is this Laura that you have so much pity for?'

Kitty had now sunk down on to a stool. 'My life-long friend,' she replied, tears still flowing. 'Sister,

I know her family as well as my own. Decent hard-working people they are. Surely you too have friends that you would not wish a tragedy like this to fall on?'

'Right, get yourself out of your theatre gown. Have a shower and then take the rest of your shift as time off.' Sister now turned to Mr Lawson. 'Anderson's grandmother died a few days ago and I think with what...' She hesitated as she glanced towards the trolley and as she looked down on the lifeless face of the pretty young woman her demeanour softened. It was obvious that she too was moved to compassion for all who would be affected by this brutal death. Sister's eyes now pleaded with Mr Lawson before she added, 'A few hours' respite to be with her relatives and friends is...'

She didn't have to finish what she was about to say. Mr Lawson just nodded and Sister went to his back and before she untied his theatre gown she gave his shoulder a light pat.

By the time Kitty had got herself washed, calmed down and into her outdoor clothes a police car had arrived at the front door of the hospital. The detective who jumped out was none other than Mark Bolan, the son of a man who had been a buddy of Kitty's late grandfather.

'Where are you going at this hour?' he asked.

'Up to my friend Laura's. You see her sister-in-law Edna ... well she was brought in but we couldn't ... we just couldn't.'

'Oh Kitty, I'm here because I'm wondering what the Edna lassie's husband is going to be charged with and I'm hoping it won't be...'

'Murder?'

Mark hated that word, and how. The uttering of the word was so destructive, not only for the victim, but to all concerned in the case. Mark was well past his thirty years' service in the force and the truth was that he should have been retired and enjoying his detective sergeant's pension. However, the war made it necessary for the older, experienced men, like him, to stay on until the young ones came home and got trained up. People, he thought to himself, think that you get used to the awful things that you see. Nae chance. I mean I've spent my whole thirty-one years in the Leith and Gayfield Divisions – took me four years to transfer into the C.I.D. and seven years to make sergeant. He laughed to himself when he thought that if he had not had a liking for having a wee dram in every hostelry he visited he probably would have made inspector. He shuddered, but on a night like this when it is the people you went to school with, worked with, shared a nip or two with, the job still twisted your guts and you wished you could throw the rule book out of the window. And tonight, a young lad just back from the war, and he goes and commits a crime ... a crime that probably will result in – oh dear God in heaven, I'm forgetting I'll have to go and tell his mother, Nessie. Nifty Nessie, whom I've stripped the willow with in umpteen church halls and ballrooms – and what will I say when she asks – I mean is there any way of softening the blow?

Before he could continue, Kitty interrupted his thoughts by saying, 'Sergeant Bolan, Edna was dead on arrival. To be truthful she would have been dead within thirty seconds of her artery being...'

'Oh, that wasn't what I wanted to hear. And I don't doubt you but I will now have to go inside to be advised officially and then ... go and inform Edna's mother and poor Nessie.'

Kitty's mouth was now dry and so her voice cracked when she pleaded, 'Sergeant, I know it's not usual procedure but could I come with you? You see there are no buses now and I would like to be with Laura and her Mum when you break the news.'

Mark Bolan didn't hesitate. The breaking of this rule he could cope with so he opened up the back door of the car to let Kitty in before he and his accompanying detective constable entered the hospital for the official notification.

When they arrived at Primrose Street Kitty stayed within the police car. It wasn't that she did not feel sympathy for Edna's mother, of course she did, but as she really didn't know Judy Fox that well, it was felt that her attending with the sergeant and constable would not only have been against police regulations but an imposition.

A long agonising half hour passed for Kitty, before the police felt that they could safely leave Edna's family. In that time Kitty thought, *Aye, it's the 22nd of June, one of the longest days in the year, and this one will also be one of the longest nights.*

When Mark and the constable eventually entered the car Kitty asked, 'How is Judy Fox and is the little girl with her?'

Mark just shrugged. He would not be answer-

95

ing the first question. How does any mother cope with the loss of her child? It was true that Edna was what in Leith was known as a "fast piece" but then her mother had hardly been a good example. Nevertheless she was a mother and now she had lost her daughter in horrific circumstances and closure for her would not come until after the trial. Mark tutted again. He knew from experience that this would be a sensational trial, not only because of Eric's dreadful action, but also because of Edna's questionable reputation. He kept continuously tutting whilst thinking of the meal Eric's prosecuting advocate would make of this case. As to the second question he quietly replied, 'She's with Edna's mum. Maybe not the best place for her but...'

When the car finally drew up at the Stewarts' lower flat, four in a block house, in Restalrig Square, it was just after one o'clock in the morning and it was evident that the household were all abed. Mark wished he could rouse the family without disturbing all the neighbours but as there was no response to his light tapping he had to clench his large fist and bang loudly on the door. The noise was so great that not only did he awaken the Stewarts but also their three neighbouring families.

Nessie, on hearing the commotion and thinking that it was Eric returning home, possibly drunk and disorderly, rushed to open the door, dressed only in her flannelette nightgown. Switching on the light her mouth gaped when she was confronted by Mark, the constable and Kitty standing on the doorstep.

'Is there some sort of ... problem?' she stammered.

'Can we come in, Nessie? We have to talk to you,' Mark asked as he took her elbow and propelled her back into the living room.

By now a pyjama-clad Laura had joined the group. The two officers and Kitty standing there all seemed so unreal to her and she wondered if she was somehow dreaming. Ignoring the police officers she instinctively looked imploringly at Kitty and gulped before muttering, 'Please don't say something has happened to Eric. He told Mum and I,' she rumbled quickly on, 'that he was just going down to see Edna. Try and get things sorted out between them for Billy's sake. We didn't think ... we just didn't, did we mum, that it was a good idea.'

By now, Nessie was as confused as Laura but she was with it enough to think that she was improperly dressed to be talking to two men. So slowly she got up and went into the hall and lifted up her outdoor coat, which she wrapped about herself. The well-worn coat gave her a feeling of somehow being in charge of herself again and when she came back into the living room she looked directly at Mark and staring him straight in the eye she said, 'Right now. No pussyfooting about. I'm not daft so I've worked it out that you haven't come here, with Kitty in tow, to tell me it's raining ... so out with it.'

Mark was not surprised at Nessie's directness. After all, they had grown up together, gone to the same school together, had their hair bone-combed by the same school nurse. Therefore he knew that

Nessie, like himself, could hold her own because she had been educated at the school of hard knocks. All this was true but he also knew that she adored Eric, so without lowering his gaze he quietly said, 'Sorry, Nessie, but Edna is dead and we have Eric in custody.'

Laura screamed and threw herself towards Kitty, who wrapped her arms about her.

Nessie just kept staring at Mark but he did notice she was now wringing her hands. 'I take it she didn't ... drop down dead?'

Mark slowly shook his head.

Breathing in deeply, and willing the tears that were now welling not to start falling she then asked, 'And is my Eric somehow...?'

All Mark could do was nod but he had to suppress a compulsion to take her into his arms and try to comfort her.

Right then Laura broke free from Kitty and lunged towards Mark, and as she beat him on the chest she screamed, 'Please tell me he maybe hit her and she fell down ... tell me it was an accident.'

The constable was now fully aware that Mark knew this family well and that he required assistance from him so in a passionless voice that seemed to bounce off the walls and echo about the room he stated, 'She was stabbed to death. Her carotid artery severed.'

Mark glared at the young constable. He was aware he was following procedure but Mark wanted to inform Nessie gently – he gritted his teeth – because he knew that there was no easy way that you could tell a mother that her son has committed – an offence that in Scotland was punishable by hanging – a word he did not wish mentioned in this house tonight. However, there were other questions he had to ask Nessie.

'Look, Nessie,' he haltingly began, 'remember your Frank's old gutting knife? The one he spent weeks carving his initials on?'

Nessie nodded. She then went into the kitchen and Mark heard her open a drawer that she then rummaged through. Spoons, forks and knives all clinked and clinked and as time passed they clinked faster and faster and then they heard the drawer being yanked from the dresser and the contents being flung on to the floor.

Kitty was the first to get into the kitchen and kneeling down beside Nessie she asked, 'What is it you are looking for, Mrs Stewart?' She had been so busy comforting Laura she hadn't heard the sergeants question to her.

'My Frank's old gutting knife. Took it on all his fishing trips, so he did. I was going to get rid of it last year when he died but then...' Kitty grabbed hold of Nessie's hands to stop her rummaging among the cutlery. Nessie then looked into Kitty's face, and as she silently implored her, tears washed down and splashed on Kitty's hands. Nessie's next words would have seemed so out of place to most people but Kitty knew from the experience she had gained in the hospital that at times of great stress and sorrow some people just babbled nonsense so she was not surprised when Nessie continued, 'Well with Mrs Scott upstairs' man being on the trawlers it's a funny week that she doesn't hand me in two or three huddies for our tea and of course they need a good gut...' She stopped and grabbed hold of Kitty as the words she had just uttered brought it home to her that Eric had killed Edna with his dad's knife.

By now everyone was in the kitchen and Mark looked at Nessie. 'Look love,' he whispered as he knelt down on the floor beside her. 'Stop your looking. We already have it... I knew when I saw Frank's initials on the wooden handle who it belonged to.' He said no more to Nessie but he raged to himself, *Why the hell did he take that blasted knife with him? Oh God in heaven, a good prosecuting lawyer will have no problem in proving he meant to kill her ... and premeditation means he will...*

Nessie was now up off her knees and, grabbing at Mark's coat lapels, she whimpered, 'Mark, please tell me they won't ... no they just can't ... hang him?'

Mark's strong arms were now around Nessie because Kitty had jumped up to console Laura, who was screaming hysterically.

After Mark and the constable left, Laura and Kitty just sat quietly as Nessie spoke more to herself than to the girls.

Wiping some tears from her face she glanced up to the mantelpiece and gazed at the photograph that had been taken of her whole family. It had been taken just before Eric had left to fight in the war. Lovingly, she looked at Frank and herself sitting with their bairns, Eric and Laura, standing at their backs. 'It's all gone wrong, Frank. And I don't suppose people will see now that when he was wee he was frightened of everything. Remember how even his own shadow terrified him. Kept looking round at it he did and over and over he would say, "Mammy, Mammy, why is it always following me?" No quite as smart as Laura, who it was true to say was never the top of the class but she always managed to get a seat in the top row.' She softly chuckled. 'See when he was in Couper Street School he was just so terrified of Miss Dodds.' She was laughing now. 'The bitch just had to belt one of the other bairns in the class and our Eric never put a foot wrong for the rest of the week. Loved to go to Lochend Park and feed the ducks, so he did. And when you were born, Laura, he was nearly six but he always wanted a hurl in the bottom of your pram.' Nessie stopped and all that was heard was the tick, ticking of the clock until she whispered, 'He loved music. Would race into the church hall and the first thing he did was to run over to the piano, hunch his wee shoulders and giggle, before he lifted up the lid and slid his wee fingers over the keys. Accomplished he was at,' she began to sing, 'Taradumdum, Taradum- dum, Taradumdumdumdumdum.' Eyes blurred with tears, all Kitty and Laura could do was exchange a glance at each other. Nessie then con- tinued, 'Wanted a piano of his own so he did. But where would the like of us get the wherewithal for a piano?' She smiled again. 'Persuaded him I did that a moothie was just as good and I could afford that. Just loved that mouth organ, so he did, and the tunes he could play on it.' She chuckled. 'Could have given that Larry Adler and his har- monica a run for his money. That moothie went everywhere with him even to the bloody war. Heard him playing it yesterday, so I did.'

101

'You know, Mum, I remember that mouth organ too. Mind you, I don't think the one he has now was the one that you bought him when he was seven. But what I do know is he plays it just so wonderfully.'

Nessie nodded. 'Well I cannae be sitting here jawing when that kitchen floor needs washing. They polis ... what a mess they made.'

Laura was about to say to her mum that the kitchen floor requiring a wash didn't matter when Kitty put up her hand to silence her. 'Leave it be, Laura,' Kitty whispered. 'She knows she cannot do anything to help her son so she is going to keep herself busy. Wiping over the floor is something she can still do.'

Laura nodded. 'Oh Kitty, we need to get him a good lawyer but we don't have that kind of money. Even if Mum and I worked twenty hours a day we still couldn't earn enough.'

'True. But in a case like Eric's there is a pool of lawyers that get appointed by the courts.' Kitty sighed before suggesting, 'And his case is such that they will be jumping over each other to defend him.'

'Aye, big news day and someone will make a name for themselves.' She stopped. She just couldn't bring herself to audibly say, *'Because if they manage to get him a reprieve from the death...'*

'Laura, how about you and I go to bed and cuddle in together?'

Kitty waited for an answer but Laura was looking out of the window at the dawn beginning to break. 'Aye, fine, but know what I would like to do first?' Kitty shook her head. 'Just. Oh Kitty, do you remember when we were young and silly?'

Kitty chuckled before saying, 'I don't think that anyone would think us approaching twenty-one as old.'

'No. I mean when we were just fourteen and on the first of May we climbed right up to the top of Arthur's Seat so we could wash our faces in the May dew in the hope that it would make us beautiful.'

'Right waste of time that was,' Kitty quipped, trying to lift Laura's spirits.

'No it wasn't. But right now I want to climb to the top again and just watch a brilliant sun rise over our city. Look over the gleaming Firth of Forth and towards the beautiful Lothians and onwards to Fife.'

Kitty nodded. She knew that right now Laura had to have something beautiful to look at and indeed looking over their homeland from the top of Arthur's Seat was exactly what was required.

By the time Kitty and Laura got back from their trip up Arthur's Seat they only had time to snooze in the armchairs for an hour before the alarm clock going off reminded them it was time for Laura to get herself ready for work.

Stretching herself, Laura mumbled, 'Wish I still worked in the munitions factory at Craigmillar. But as I have only been working in Janis dress shop for two weeks, and I'm still sort of on probation, I'd better get myself moving.'

'Well Janis is a much nicer type of job than the munitions.'

'Right enough, Kitty, but there's no overtime and no matter how hard you work there are definitely no bonuses.'

Having got themselves organised Kitty then walked with Laura just as far as her father's house because it would have been alien to her to pass by without popping in.

As was to be expected the door was unlocked and when Kitty entered the kitchen Connie just stared.

'Not going to say something like, "I'm glad to see you"?'

'Well I know you were on night duty last night so you won't have heard ... but oh Kitty ... see when I went over to the bakers for some bran scones at seven this morning and I was told about...'

'The jungle drums working overtime, were they?'

'Honestly, Kitty, I nearly threw up when Myrtle Black described how Edna had been hacked to pieces.'

'That is a lie. It was one stab. And as the neck is soft tissue it would not have taken much force,' Kitty vehemently defended.

'Look dinnae take it out on me,' Connie huffed before simpering, 'I'm just repeating what I heard in the baker's this morning.'

'Is that so? Well tomorrow morning you will be able to put the clashing mob, who are enjoying and adding to the poor Stewart family's misery, right?' Connie meekly nodded. Kitty now on her high horse then added with such venom that her spit sprayed on to Connie, 'Don't suppose them that were making the whole sorry business worse gave a thought to Eric's mother and sister. Connie, can't you see in no way are they to blame but they are caught up in it?'

'Look before you go on taking all your frustration out on me can I say the one in all this sorry mess that my heart bleeds for is Nessie.' Kitty, now regretting berating Connie, just nodded. 'And do you know, Kitty, before you came in I was thinking of getting Dora to watch my two so I could go over and see Nessie.' Connie, still not sure that Kitty was thinking straight hesitated, 'Trouble is I'm not in the habit of calling on her. To be truthful we just meet up at the club. So you see I wouldn't want her to think I was prying.'

'Don't go this morning, you see Mark Bolan is in charge of the case and I heard him say to Nessie that he would come back this morning. Going to try, he is, to get his bosses to agree to her seeing Eric before he's taken up to the High Street court to be formally charged...'

'After that will he be allowed out on bail or does he go back to being held at Leith Police Station?'

Kitty shook her head. 'No use pretending ... he will be remanded and his crime is so serious there will be no bail ... so I'm afraid he will be held at Saughton Prison until his trial.'

'It's a to-do, right enough ... and the Stewarts are such a nice family ... sure they don't deserve this ... especially Nessie ... just getting over losing her man she is.'

'So the poor soul is. The only good thing is that after five years in the care of German hospitality being a guest at Saughton will seem, to Eric, like being lodged in a posh hotel.'

Forgetting not to repeat the street gossip Connie blundered in with, 'And folks were saying he might swing for it.'

'Connie,' Kitty blustered, 'don't say that – that is tempting fate. We have to believe that he has a fighting chance.' She moved over and grabbed Connie by the shoulders. 'Please, please try and understand I can't deal with thinking that it might end like the gossips are... Oh no, it just couldn't.' Kitty was now sobbing and all Connie could do to comfort her was to put her strong arms around her. As Kitty's tears ran down Connie's neck she mumbled, 'That happening would not only destroy Eric but it would also be impossible for Laura and her mum to live with.'

It was just after half past eight when Laura got home. When she had finished work at six o'clock Michael, her lovely loyal Tricky Mike, was waiting for her.

Before he could say anything she said, 'You will have heard about Edna and...'

'I don't think there is anybody in Leith who doesn't know or have an opinion on it.'

Laura bit into her top lip before saying, 'That will include your mum and dad.'

'Uh huh.'

'And am I still to have tea at your house tonight?' Mike's reply was to lower his head. 'Do they want you to give me up?'

'My dad doesn't. He says the war's to blame for it all ... mind you I don't know how he comes to that conclusion but ... and aye okay my mum thinks ... for just now it would be best not to be seen with you.'

'So.'

'Well I'm here and I think we should go to the chippie and have our tea because nothing will change how I feel about you, Laura, and even if my mum puts me out on the street I'll still court you.'

Her mum saying, 'Have you eaten?' brought Laura back to the present.

'Aye, Mike met me and we had a chippie.' She shrugged her shoulders and gave a little giggle in the hope that it would lift her mum's spirits. 'And like two bairns we sat in Taylor Gardens sharing a supper and a single fish.'

'So his folks are not going to get him to give...'

'No, Mum, they are nice people. Now let's forget about Mike and me, how did things go?'

'Well we have a lot to thank God for.'

Laura couldn't see just what, but as her mother's faith meant so much to her, and that would be the thing that would see her through whatever was to come, she just nodded.

'Mark took me in to see Eric. Quiet as he usually is, he was. And Laura, they have appointed a solicitor sort of advocate man for him. Young lad but keen and bright ... but they have to be very clever to be solicitors, don't they?'

'They do, Mum. And did Eric have anything to say?'

'Just that his lawyer's name is Bill Gracie and that he wants you and me to bring up wee Billy.'

Laura could not help but frown.

Noticing Laura's reluctance Nessie quickly

added, 'I know there have been rumours that Billy was not Eric's but today Laura, God let me see the proof that he is.' Laura's eyes widened. 'Aye, Connie Anderson and I took Billy and her two to play in the hall. Honestly, I could have screamed when our Billy went over and lifted the piano lid up and started tinkering on the keys. Then on our way home just to make sure, but I needed no proof, I bought him a wee mouthie.' Nessie stretched forward to grasp Laura's arm as she emphasised, 'Laura, the wee soul can blow on it already. Now is that not all the proof we need?'

Laura nodded. It was true people like herself were better educated and therefore they asked more in-depth questions than the simple ones that her mum did. And she really did hope that Billy was indeed Eric's son, but that would not matter to her mother and herself now. No matter what anybody else said, wee Billy was one of them – a true Stewart through and through.

# PART THREE

## JULY 1945

Whenever Kitty and Laura entered Kitty's dad's house they threw themselves down on the couch.

'You two look how I feel ... all in,' remarked Connie with a long sigh.

Kitty bolted herself upright so she could get a better look at Connie. Immediately she could see that her miscarriage of two weeks ago had taken its toll. She never said, but Kitty and her Aunt Kate thought that trailing around the Wider Granton constituency, pushing leaflets through doors, begging people to hang posters in their windows and forever talking to women in the shops, at the school gates, on the street corners, had been the main contributor to Connie losing her baby. It was true that when she had first discovered that she was pregnant she had been far from happy but when the little life died within her she somehow felt that she had been robbed. There was also the deep regret that when she had found herself pregnant again she had said that she could have done without another mouth to feed. Kitty also remembered that when Connie had returned home from her brief stay in Bruntsfield Women's Only Hospital, her first remark to Kitty was, 'I know I said I didn't want him, but I did. You see, I am just so sure that the wee soul would've been a son. And I would have liked that. Because I would have felt that I had, in some way, given your dad his darling Jack back.'

Moved emotionally by these remarks Kitty had blundered in with, 'I know you can never be a substitute mother for our Bobby because he was away from home when you and dad got married. But you and Dad still have Davy at home.' Connie huffed and it was then that Kitty realised that Davy was now eighteen years old and it was true that he liked Connie but she was not the woman who had given him birth – the mother, like Kitty, he remembered and loved so much that no one could ever replace her. A little smile had then flicked on to Kitty's face and taking Connie's hand in hers she quietly said, 'Connie, we are forgetting that there is one thing that everybody appreciates about you and Dad getting married and that is that at last Rosebud has a mother. And you are doing such a great job with her. Indeed she and wee Jackie will always be not only sisters but best pals too.'

That was all two weeks ago. Today everyone was worn out. Johnny had expected that everybody would work themselves into the ground to get him voted into parliament. He hoped they all realised that he desperately needed to have a purpose in life. Needed to be earning enough to keep his family and his head above water. He never said to Connie, or anybody else for that matter, how he felt about Connie losing the baby. It was as if nothing was to come between him and his winning the election. To be fair to him he did manage to rearrange his schedule so he could go into Bruntsfield Hospital to visit Connie. However, on the downside, he only managed to sit, not still but agitated, for a full half an hour. Kitty was also at Connie's bedside during his visit and she was more than a bit put out when all that seemed to be concerning her father was that the Conservatives were cocksure of not only winning the election but doing so with an increased majority. In a voice that was laden with ridicule Kitty had suggested that before he threw in the towel it might be a good idea to wait and hear what the result was.

It was true that Kitty was utterly exhausted. This was because she had done more than her bit in canvassing for her father. Even today, when she had been so tired that when she had finished her early shift at the hospital all she wished to do was go to bed. But no, she was duty bound, according to her father, to do one last round of electioneering. She was so fed up that she vowed that should her father be elected and later stand for a second term she would volunteer for the foreign legion or whatever just as long as she didn't have to hand out another poster or knock on another door. She smiled. Grateful she was that after today helping her dad would be over and she would have time again for everyone else that was important in her life. Still staring at Connie she was about to suggest that she pull herself together when Laura took the initiative.

'Connie,' Laura diplomatically began, 'is your hair tied up in that dull turban because you've just washed it?'

Shaking her head Connie pulled the scarf from

her hair. Kitty immediately became concerned because she could see that Connie had not shampooed her locks for some time.

'Just cannae be bothered to do anything really,' Connie whimpered. 'I cook, clean and shop but by the time I've bedded the bairns I just want to sit and...'

'Bubble,' suggested Kitty.

Holding back the tears Connie nodded. 'I'm useless. If it wasn't for Dora downstairs and Laura's mum ... och... I'm such a mess I need them to keep the cruelty man from taking Rosebud and Jackie away and putting them into a home.'

'Into a home!' exploded Kitty. 'Don't be daft.' Kitty swallowed and mellowed her tone before going over and laying her hands on Connie's shoulders. 'Look, I've seen this before. You are not failing. It is just that women who lose a baby get what's called "the baby blues" and okay with all that has been going on ... and my Dad not being around much to support you, perhaps ... and only perhaps, you've got a bad dose of it. But starting right now I'm going to run you a bath and Laura, who should really be a hairdresser, is going to wash your hair.'

Somebody bothering, trying to understand, should have had a calming effect on Connie but it only succeeded in upsetting her further. Through choking sobs she snivelled, 'The two of you will be good ones if you can because the fire has not been lit today so there's no hot water. There's only a sliver of Palmolive soap left and not enough Derbac to wash my eyebrows.'

'Is that right? And I hope you think that will stop Laura and me getting you bathed and your hair washed. No chance ... just inconveniences that can be got rid of, so they are. Right, Laura, come on, help me to get the pots and kettle filled up and on to the cooker. Then we will fill up the clothes boiler. And Connie, as you are not lousy we won't be requiring the Derbac soap, and to get your locks washed I will just dissolve a teaspoonful of "A One Soap Powder" in a jam jar. Then a final rinse with chip-shop vinegar. Oh aye, not only does it taste great on your chips but it fairly makes your hair shine!'

'Aye, and do you know something, Connie, uptown hairdressers, when they do what Kitty is going to do to your hair, they call it shampooing and conditioning?'

The girls both tittered and laughed as they raised their hands to bob their own hair.

'But why are you bothering?'

'Because tomorrow Aunty Kate will be baby-sitting here and you will be at the counting station standing beside my dad and there is no way I could allow you to go there looking like Betsy the Rag Woman.'

'That also means that your crossover overall and these thick lisle thread stockings will be getting an overdue holiday?' Laura said whilst untying Connie's overall from the back.

'You've got it in one, Laura.' Kitty then turned her attention back to Connie. 'Don't suppose you have any nylon stockings?'

Connie shook her head.

'Right I'll lend you a pair for tomorrow.'

'Where did you get them?'

'From an American soldier whose nose I put two stitches in. But, as they are fifteen denier to die for, I want them back ... and with no snags or rips.'

Laura laughed uproariously before gurgling, 'Here, Kitty, since when has Connie had such long locks?' She then lifted up a handful of Connie's thick hair and as she began curling it through her fingers she mumbled, 'Think since you have so much of it I will set it up in a victory roll.'

Kitty's reply was a wicked nod and a wink.

It was past midnight when Johnny finally got home. Everyone was abed. He firstly felt a bit miffed that Connie had not sat up for him. But as he lowered himself into his comfy armchair he was glad he was alone with time to think. Something he had perfected of late was talking to himself and his thoughts were now on the last couple of months.

It had been some roller coaster, the run-up to the election. To be honest the accident that had made the amputation of his left forearm necessary had not only resulted in the loss of that limb but also his self-confidence. It was true that Robbs, the shipyards where he had spent all his working life, firstly as an apprentice and then as a fully qualified plater, did try to find him a job that he could do. But if he was being honest, watching to see that the men were only clocking themselves in was not only demeaning to him but it was against his trade-union principles to spy on his brother workers.

Refusing the job in Robbs had meant that he had to go, cap in hand, to the union and ask for a job. And they did find him one, one where he did the mediating in disputes that broke out in all the industries in and around Leith. He did like that job and he was very good at it but the pay was only half of what he had earned in the shipyards. To him, watching Connie scrimp and scrape on his reduced earnings was humiliating. This being so he made up his mind that he would have to win the seat in parliament so he could hold his head up again – honestly earn a living wage so that he could suitably provide for his family. He accepted that he was not intellectually brilliant but he was above average, and where he scored was that he had more than his fair share of common sense. He was also, where his fellow man was concerned, caring and sympathetic and when having to give out news that the workers didn't wish to hear, he used his diplomacy skills to put it over.

Today he had been at the gates of the factories before seven and he had tried his best to persuade people to vote for him. Tomorrow he had to accept the will of the people. If he lost he could do no more than stand back and let the bus go by. But if he won, and please God, he pleaded, let that be the outcome, I will again have some power – be a man who commands respect – be someone that the people trust and listen to.

Thursday the 5th July was a long, tiresome and worrying day. It was a foregone conclusion that Hoy would win in the Leith seat. Wider Granton was well ... all day Johnny tried to keep control of his emotions and a count of who was voting for him. But some of the residents in Wider Granton kept to themselves, as they were entitled to do, who they had voted for. However, Johnny grudgingly accepted that the upper class saw no need for change, but the workers, the men and women who had worked and fought in the war, were now demanding social change so perhaps...?

He just had time to whisper the result in Connie's ear before he and the other candidates were called up to the rostrum where the winning candidate and votes would be announced. Connie, thanks to Kitty and Laura, who were also in the hall, was looking good, but when she started to cry Laura and Kitty rushed over to support her. Both girls thought the worst and then they had to keep quiet whilst the votes for each candidate were announced. When Johnny's count was called out Kitty slumped to the floor – he had not only won but by the national average of forty-seven per cent of the vote. The Conservatives' candidate was second with thirty-six per cent and the Liberal could only enjoy nine per cent.

Everyone seemed to be able to get to Johnny to shake his hand except his own family, but that didn't matter to them. He had won. For Connie it was a dream come true. She truly believed the old Johnny that she had fallen so hopelessly in love with would now be reborn. Oh yes, the husband, father and brother that she and the family loved so well would now be able to come to terms with his disability and re-emerge as a whole person.

The party spirit that had spontaneously erupted on Victory in Europe day started up again in Leith when it became clear that not only had James Hoy won the Leith seat with a staggering sixty-one per cent voting for him but also that one of their own sons, Johnny Anderson, had taken the dubious seat of Wider Granton.

As the rejoicing started up again the people truly believed that at last social change would come. They would see in the lifetime of the Labour Government a fairer society – the bringing in of a just society that included a Welfare State and a National Health Service.

When the immediate and wider Armstrong clan arrived back at Restalrig, Connie immediately dragged the large cooking pot full of tripe, potatoes and onions on to heat. She knew that the day and night would be long and at the end of it all her family would require sustenance. She had therefore reckoned that what her hungry family would need, whether Johnny won or lost, was a big comforting bowl of Leith's very own cheap delicacy – tripe and onions.

Four weeks later anyone standing on the platform where the ten o'clock train to London was about to depart would have thought that a senior member of the Royal Family was about to board. However, it was just that all of Johnny's immediate and wider family, along with some close friends, had gathered to wave him off. They of course only had platform tickets and they cheered when Johnny boarded the train brandishing his House of Commons Member of Parliament rail pass – this gesture was just to emphasise that he really was on his way in more ways than one.

It had been a long four weeks for Johnny since he was voted in as Member of Parliament for Wider Granton and he was more than eager to get on with his new job. Nonetheless, he had to mark time as the final results of the General Election were not known until 26th of July 1945 when Churchill resigned as Prime Minister and Clement Attlee was summoned to the palace and invited by King George VI to form a Labour administration.

To be truthful, the weeks whilst he was waiting had not been wasted. Connie had insisted on taking him down to the "Fifty Shillings Tailor", where he was fitted out with a suit and a hat, known as an Anthony Eden. Connie reckoned that if this hat was mandatory for a Conservative posh boy then Johnny would just have to have one too.

Johnny had gulped when he realised the expense that had to be lavished on his clothing for his new job. Then when Connie had suggested to him that he ask Kate if she could advance him some of the three hundred pounds that she was due to pay him, for the third of the house that his mother had left him, he humphed, hawed and spluttered.

It was true that his mum's house had been valued at a staggering nine hundred pounds. Kate naturally wished to stay in the house that had been her home for nearly twenty years but she also wished to be fair to her brother. However, three hundred pounds she and Hans did not have at the present time. They did offer to pay so much a week but Johnny felt that way his mother's legacy to him would just be filtered away on housekeeping and rent. The second offer to pay the amount in full in eighteen months' time was accepted by Johnny. What he had not divulged to Kate was that in the biscuit tin that his mother had left him there was a large envelope marked, "Johnny's Own Doorstep Fund". This was, of course, Jenny's way of reinforcing what she was always encouraging Johnny to do – start saving so that one day he could purchase a home of his own. Renting, Jenny always said, was fine but everyone should be trying to buy their own home. Unfortunately the ninety-five pounds, all saved in ten-shilling notes over a period of years, he had to use, not to buy a house, but to pay rent arrears to Edinburgh Corporation and thus keep a roof over his family's head, food, heating and new clothes and bedding for the children. Not a penny of it was left when he humbled himself, as he saw it, to ask Kate for fifty pounds advance from what she owed him.

The train had steamed out of the Waverley and everyone was still waving when Johnny settled down with his morning newspaper. He would never be able to remember what the headline story was that day because his thoughts were back with his mum and he silently promised her that when Kate paid over the two hundred and fifty pounds balance of what she still owed him he would have saved up enough to enable himself to go and "buy" the dream his mother always had for him. Now, sitting watching the countryside pass by he was fascinated. Then he would be because he had never been further west than Glasgow or south of

119

North Berwick. His thoughts had then turned to Connie. She had been very down since she had lost their baby and it was true she was better but not quite back to her usual jovial self. As the train carried him further away he vowed that he would take care of her, believe in her as she had in him. A smug smile then drifted across his face as he thought, *If I do well she will be so proud of me and it will have been all her and my mother's doing.*

# PART FOUR

## AUGUST 1945

Connie had just taken charge of the key to Kate's home when she hesitated and put her hand over Kate's. 'Hope it all goes well for you and Hans.' Connie was referring to the fact that Kate and Hans were now on their way down to Kendal in the Lake District to visit a house and, if everything went according to plan, they would come home with a Jewish orphan who, as far as everyone in Leith was concerned, would be their adopted son.

Kate recalled that as far back as July when she and Hans had been blackmailed into putting off their visit to Hans' cousin, Josef, in the south of England, until after the General Election, they had been making enquiries about giving a home to a Jewish orphan who had survived the Holocaust.

Firstly Hans had contacted Josef by letter at the establishment he was working at down Dover way. Josef was so delighted to hear from Hans that as soon as was possible he had travelled up by train to meet up with him. This was because as far as he knew, or at least believed, Hans was his only relative to have survived the war.

When Josef had indicated that he would travel to Edinburgh just as soon as he could Hans had been a bit apprehensive about his visit. He just didn't know how Josef would react to Hans now having remarried and more so to someone outwith their faith. All his concerns turned out to be unfounded. Josef immediately took to Kate. Now this surprised Hans because Kate, whom he knew would never, not even to please him, convert to the Jewish faith because she was so comfortable with her own faith, completely entranced Josef. Indeed before he left after his two-day visit Josef was convinced that she would be an ideal person to take on a troubled and abused child who appeared to have no living relative. It was true that the British Government had agreed to take in more than its quota of the rescued children. And at this present time they were now in the process of bringing as many as they could to Britain. It was hoped that all of the younger children would find new homes. The older children, late teenagers, would be placed in hostels and supported educationally and financially until they could provide for themselves.

On their arrival in Britain the younger children were taken, with the help of the Red Cross, and housed in large boarding type houses all over the country and Josef had suggested that Hans and Kate should visit the home just outside Kendal.

During his visit Hans had said to Josef that he was keen to adopt a child but Josef had said that in the first instance this would not be possible. The reason for this was that there was a possibility that in time, perhaps several years, contact between surviving members of families could happen. This situation had been caused by the momentous scale of chaos among the Jewish population deliberately created by the Nazis in their desire to rid the world of Judaism. 'What I am saying,' Josef had gone on to emphasise to Hans and Kate, 'is some relative might, in years to come, arrive to claim the child you are caring for. Now admit it, it would be only just and correct that every assistance would be given to reunite the child with his blood family.' He hesitated before adding, 'But that should not put you off taking a child on a substitute "aunt and uncle" basis – but right now that is all that is on offer. Look, the scale of the horror is such that most of these surviving children will never be lucky enough to be found by one of their own blood relatives. So as the two of you have so much to offer a child, I say take a chance, and go on and foster. Believe me, having been with the two of you for the last two days I am convinced that you will be so successful that the child will come to see you as mother and father.'

Not being able to adopt any of the surviving children had come as a complete shock to Hans and Kate. They were further upset when Josef had gone on to say that the fostering of a child was on – he did struggle to find kinder words but in the end could only come up with a sale or return basis. This was because people did not understand just how difficult raising a child who had been so traumatised by the horrors they had witnessed, still affected by the medical experiments carried out on them, the brutal starvation they had endured, would be. Josef's voice cracked with emotion when he finally said, 'Two young lads had been "uncled and auntied" five times. You see the poor children had formed bonds with each other in the concentration camp and they could not, and would not, settle unless they were together.'

Hans calling, 'Kate, Kate, you're standing there dreaming and we should be getting off' put an instant end to her reminiscence and contemplations.

'Right enough,' she replied with a short laugh. 'As neither of us is really acquainted with the route we'd better get off.' Taking her hand from Connie's she said, 'Thanks for looking after my cat.' Connie nodded and both women then looked over the road to where Nessie was trying to persuade Rosebud and Billy that it was not a good idea to start knocking lumps out of each other. Looking at Nessie, who seemed to have aged ten years since Eric had been charged with murder, Kate whispered to Connie, 'How are things going...?'

Connie instinctively understood that Kate was asking if there was any further news on Eric's trial. Not wishing Nessie to hear she lifted her hand and placed it over her mouth before murmuring, 'Trial date is being set for September. Poor Nessie has been up to high doh since she was told. That's why I got her to tag along with me today ... she needs someone just to blether to her about nothing.'

'Right enough,' Kate agreed, 'a cup of tea and a wee chat takes your mind off things.'

When Kitty started her training in Leith Hospital in early 1944 she was so anxious to make the grade that she was forever asking questions of anyone she deemed to be further on in their career than she was. Somehow she had managed to get a nurse's pocket dictionary and it became her saviour as she tried to not only memorise how to say the medical terminology but also understand what it meant. That was all then. Now she was halfway through her three years' training she found herself still clutching the textbook that had cost her fifteen shillings. This book she hoped would help her to pass the exam that was looming. She just had to pass it but she was so unsure of her ability that she put off forking out on some new uniform black lacing shoes.

It was now her break time and she thought she would spend it sitting in Taylor Gardens reading the textbook and as her mind was on nothing else but the looming exam she screamed and started to run when Dr Dougal McNeil jumped out of a side corridor and shouted, 'Boo'.

Unfortunately, Matron was just ahead of her and when Kitty's running feet drew level with her she turned and hissed. 'Anderson, may I remind you that in my hospital no one runs unless there is a fire or someone has haemorrhaged.'

Kitty gulped as she bowed her head and fled through the entrance doors. Once she was seated in Taylor Gardens Dougal had the temerity to come and sit beside her.

'Look,' she hissed, 'just go away. I am preparing for my exam and I don't want to be disturbed ... especially by a halfwit.'

Reaching over, and taking her hand in his, Dougal sought to have her look at him. 'Look, Kitty,' he began sincerely, 'you don't need to bother with exams. I'm going home to Canada in six months' time and what I want is to take you with me as my wife.'

'Have you had a blow to your head?'

Dougal shook his head. 'Never been saner. You are the only girl for me. I know that and I am therefore offering to marry you and whisk you off to a new life in Canada.'

Kitty then started to chuckle with such vigour that her whole body shook. 'Well, as tempting as your offer is,' she mocked, 'my ambition is to finish my training. Then do my obligatory one year as a staff nurse here and I cannot allow even a proposition as enticing as yours, to get in the way.'

'So you are turning me down?'

Kitty shrugged. Then with a mischievous smile she nudged Dougal as she replied, 'Of course a girl would need to be out of her mind to turn down a proposal of marriage from you. So what I am saying is that I have to finish my training, honour the contract I made with the hospital when I started, then and only then would I be happy to consider...'

Dougal was now down on his bended knee. He was so pleased that he didn't seem to notice that he was kneeling on the wet grass. 'You mean we can start courting now and in two – at the most three – years' time you will come to Canada?'

She nodded... She would like to have said no because he was such a flirt. But she grudgingly admitted that he was the most bewitching man she had ever met. He completely entranced her and it was like a dream come true that he wished to marry her – spend the rest of his life with her – be faithful to her and her alone. But the one thing that life had taught Kitty was that no one was promised tomorrow and if anything happened to Dougal after they were married she would have to be employable – able to earn enough money to keep herself and any children that they might have. So even though it annoyed her as much as him, she would finish her training – besides she loved her job and would not wish to do any other.

It was just before lunch when Kate and Hans drew up in front of the large house that obviously had at one time been the dwelling place of a very wealthy family.

When Kate pulled the bell of The Larches it clanged so loudly that she quickly jumped back and landed on top of Hans' feet.

They were just recovering from their mishap when the door was opened by a middle-aged lady with a face that radiated and a smile that bewitched.

'I do so hope that you are Mr and Mrs Busek?' she almost sang as she offered her hand to Kate and then Hans. 'I am Eva Vasor. Your cousin, Josef, said he thought that you would probably arrive in time for lunch.'

'Josef is here? Hans asked as he peered into the hallway.

'No. No. We spoke on the telephone yesterday. And today he will be meeting some of the three hundred children who will be arriving on three Lancaster bombers today and tomorrow.'

The inside of the house, although stripped of its original furnishings, with the exception of a baby grand piano, amazed Kate. The whole of her home back in Edinburgh could have fitted into the hall and the large sitting room, which had now been turned into a classroom.

'You teach the children here?' Hans asked as his eyes roamed the room.

'Not formal teaching as you would have known. But the children, in most cases we sadly think, will make their home here in Britain, therefore it is essential that they speak English.' She tittered, 'You will be surprised at just how quickly they learn our language.'

Hans nodded and with a sly smile he looked directly at the piano and quipped, 'So piano lessons are not on the curriculum?'

'Not at the moment and that is simply because we do not have anyone on our teaching staff with these skills. Nonetheless, should any child wish to play the instrument, then they are at liberty, no encouraged, to do so.'

'And do any of them try?'

'Last week a boy was transferred from one of our other homes and he just loves to tickle the ivories. He's not skilled because naturally he has had no lessons of late but there is something magical about his playing. Now there's something... I must have him play a little medley for you before you go.' She hesitated. 'Do either of you play?'

Kate shook her head but Hans nodded and he sidled over to the instrument. Once he had sat down on the piano stool he lifted the lid and his fingers began to expertly run over the keys. The room was then filled with a selection of the music of Irving Berlin. His rendering of 'White Christmas' did not seem to anyone listening to be out of place. They all knew Christmas was four months away and they were in a Jewish home where Christmas would not be celebrated but the haunting melody didn't seem out of place because in this house all that the children had left were dreams – dreams that for a few might come true, but not in the way they truly wished.

Before meeting any of the children, whom they might wish to foster, Eva suggested that they had lunch. Lunchtimes in this house meant that all the children and the staff sat down and ate together.

Eva had explained that the food being served to the children was nutritious but because they had been starved for so long it had to be simple. This was not a problem to Kate or Hans because they themselves preferred homely fare. Kate then just sat with her hands relaxed in her lap while the religious blessings and rituals that she was used to Hans doing before he ate were over.

The chicken noodle soup was delicious and it was followed by strawberry blancmange with a few fresh strawberries. Whilst Kate was finishing her dessert she found herself gazing at a child she reckoned to be somewhere between the ages of four and five. What had first attracted her to the child was that she seemed to be the only female child, however, it turned out that there were another three girls among the twenty-five children being housed at The Larches. When she asked Eva as to why there was such an imbalance of gender among the children, Eva just shrugged before whispering, 'There are reasons that fewer girls survived. Not something I think we should discuss here.' Eva hesitated before adding, 'But could I repeat that today, and for the next few days, your Josef and his associates will be welcoming three Lancaster bombers who will be flying in from Prague. They are bringing a further three hundred children who have survived and just eighty of these are girls.'

Kate nodded. She was no fool and obviously more boys survived because they were physically more able for slave labour. Her eyes strayed to the little girl again. There was something about her that disturbed Kate. It was not because her eyes appeared lifeless – yes they were that – but it was something much deeper. There was a haunting despondency and bleakness about the emaciated child. Even her hair looked sickly, anaemic and lifeless. It slowly dawned on Kate that the child still breathed but she was dead. The poor little girl was so damaged that she was incapable of communicating even with the other children.

After lunch Hans and Kate were going to have to decide which child they were going to offer a home to. Hans had already made up his mind it would be a boy – no way, he told Kate, could he bear to replace Dalia his little daughter – the child of his heart who would always be the flower of his eye.

From the moment Hans was introduced to Amos Kramer there was an immediate chemistry between them. And although he did individually meet several other boys, his mind was made up. Turning to Eva Vasor he said, 'I think that Amos, the first boy I met, would fit into our family life well so I think you should make the necessary arrangements for my wife and I to take on responsibility for him.'

Eva bent closer to Hans and she smiled before asking, 'Would you consider taking on two boys?'

Hans and Kate were taken aback and looked at each other to see what reaction this suggestion had on each other. Kate was the first to shake her head and as Hans followed he replied, 'No. You see we are really what is considered middle-aged and my wife has never had a child so I think one child would be our limit.'

Kate would always remember how quickly Eva's facial expression turned from hopeful to completely crestfallen.

The silence in the room was deafening. Eventually Eva slowly uttered, 'I am afraid that Amos Kramer would only agree to you fostering him provided you also took on Benjamin Sisken.'

Kate and Hans exchanged a knowing look with each other. Hans then looked at Eva full on and said, 'I take it that you have tried, let's say a few times, to settle the boys but they have always been brought back because they cannot settle away from each other?'

Eva hesitated before answering. 'Well not from this home but you see they were housed firstly in two houses in the Dover area and there were several good people who wished to take the boys on singly ... but they only survived in the concentration camp because they looked out for each other and they...' Eva threw her hands up in despair. 'They are completely ill at ease apart. I have been asked...'

Hans interrupted, 'By my cousin Josef who

brought them here a few days ago.'

Eva nodded. 'After Josef met your wife and yourself he was convinced that you would be able to give the two boys a home.'

Giving each other a look that acknowledged they had been set up Hans shook his head. 'No. Not even for Josef could I take on two.' He now turned to Kate and he allowed his eyes that had always mesmerised her and had her do his bidding and said, 'It would be too much for us, wouldn't it, my dear?'

Kate knew her husband and she knew that he wished to take Amos on and the deal on offer was that they would also have to take Benjamin. If she was being truthful, the visit to the The Larches and the observing of the little girl had completely distressed her. So much so that she was not really capable of making a rational decision, but she loved Hans and he needed to be doing something to help his distressed country people. So even though she had doubts, grave doubts, about her being able to cope, she found herself saying, 'Hans, let's take the two boys home. Only one proviso ... and that is that you won't make any difference between them.'

Eva looked at Hans in a quizzical manner. Hans replied, 'I have to make no favourites. It is a failing of mine, very rarely mind you, to be a tiny bit biased.'

Kate huffed before rolling her eyes and surveying the ceiling.

Hans and Kate stayed the night at The Larches getting to know Amos and Ben, as he liked to be known. Very early in the morning they were soon all packed up and the car had just taken off and reached the end of the long driveway when Kate shouted, 'Hans, stop!'

Pulling up so abruptly resulted in the boys being jolted out of their seats and Hans had to turn round to make sure that they were not injured. Having assured himself that the boys were okay he turned back to face Kate. 'What on earth is wrong with you?' he hissed.

'Hans,' she cried as tears spilled over, 'I am so sorry but I just can't do it. We must go back. I have to be able to live...'

'But we agreed.'

'Yes we did but it was to salve your conscience but ... Hans ... take my word for it we have to go back.'

Amos and Ben looked from one to the other. Amos then leaned forward and placed his hand on Hans' shoulder. 'It's okay by us, just turn the car and go back.'

Clenching his hands into fists Hans bent his head so that Kate could not see what her decision meant to him. Slowly he allowed his hands to relax and he started up the car again. His first instinct was to go forward in the hope that Kate would change her mind. But he knew Kate all too well so he could do nothing but make a three point turn and head the car back to The Larches.

As soon as the car pulled up Kate jumped out and raced up to the door and hauled on the bell. As she waited to be admitted she turned to look at Hans and the boys who were already out of the car and assembling the boys' few belongings. 'What on earth are you doing, Hans?' she hollered.

'Well now that we,' his voice was clipped with anger, 'no *you* have decided you do not wish to foster the boys.'

'I never said that.'

'Then why are we not on our way home?'

Before Kate could answer Eva was standing at the open doorway. The expression on her face was anything but friendly. She had acknowledged that Kate and Hans might find the rearing of Amos and Ben too difficult but she was hardly prepared to have them brought back within five minutes.

'You are having second thoughts?'

'I am. Look, Eva, please understand, I just have tried...' Eva's derisive laugh astonished Kate but she decided to ignore it and went on to say, 'I didn't sleep well last night ... you see I once lost...'

'We all lost in that bloody war. The poor children here more so than anybody,' Eva protested.

Hans had now come to stand on the step beside Kate and he and Eva's jaws dropped in unison when Kate uttered, 'That's what I mean. Please allow us to take the little mute girl.'

Again in unison Eva and Hans gasped, 'Instead of Amos and Ben?'

'Good heavens, no! Along with...' Kate's eyes flashed with anger. And turning to Hans and pointing to Eva she spat, 'She doesn't know me but you do, so how could you think I would not do everything I could to make fostering the boys work?'

Hans bowed his head in shame.

Eva said, 'Look Kate, come in and let me explain about the little girl ... Aliza.'

The two women then got themselves seated in the two small armchairs strategically placed in the bay window to give a view of the beautiful, peaceful garden. However, Eva noted that the tranquil, scenic view was not having a calming influence on Kate. Both she and Hans were surprised at Kate's reaction as she always appeared to be in complete control and self-possessed in any situation.

'Kate,' Eva began, 'I accept that Aliza Stein has awakened a mothering instinct within you but ... I am sorry to say that Aliza is so damaged that you would be more than likely to fail in...' Eva hesitated. She knew what she had to say but the kind of words she wished to use to soften the message seemed to be evading her. After a tense few minutes she added, 'The child has had everything that she loved and felt safe with taken from her. Her parents are long gone. Everyone that was part of her very first years has disappeared. She has even lost her native language. People are speaking to her in words that are absolutely foreign to her ears. I have tried to get through to her ... she is able to speak but she does not converse.' Eva shook her head. 'Please believe me, Kate, I have tried and tried to communicate with her ... but she does not respond.'

Kate by now had stopped plucking at her skirt and she bent over and placed her hand on Eva's knee. 'I am aware of all that. Now please listen to me. I was raised within, and still belong, to a family who support each other through whatever. What I am saying is that I have known and assisted my brother and his children through great sorrow so I know how long it takes for psychological wounds to heal. Look, Eva, if Aliza is to have any chance, and I'm not saying I will succeed, oh no I'm not saying that, what I am saying is that there is the probability I won't, but you have to allow me to try. Eva,' Kate now took Eva's hand in hers, 'you and I both know that it is a big, bad world out there and people like to take on children that are cute and handsome. So until Aliza grows some hair, some flesh on her bones and starts to speak and, God bless her, perhaps starts to look cute and pretty, she won't...'

An uncomfortable few minutes ticked by before Eva unconsciously placed her other hand over Kate's. Her grip was so intense that Kate winced. Both women then looked directly into the eyes of each other and tears surfaced. In unison they turned to look into the far corner of the room where a little mute girl was pressing herself hard against the wall. Both women knew that this was Aliza's way of trying to make herself invisible.

Laura sensually pursed her generous lips to even out the fresh coat of lipstick that she had just applied. Then giving the coat of Max Factor pan make-up on her cheeks a little pat she turned to Kitty. 'Well,' she began with a sigh, 'it is true that some of us weren't born beautiful but thanks to Max Factor we can appear so.'

'You could be right. You know my mum never went to bed without plastering her face with Pond's Cold Cream and in the morning she couldn't eat her porridge until she had lathered another coat of cold cream on.' Kitty sighed. Her mum had been dead for nearly six years now but it still hurt to think of her. To Kitty she had embodied all that a woman should be. Her skin had been just so perfect that Kitty thought that Pond's should have paid her mum to advertise their wares.

Kitty was still thinking of her Mum when Laura waggled her tongue around her mouth before saying, 'Here, Kitty, that Dougal you brought to the dancing tonight ... he's quite a dish ... and he's a doctor.' Laura laughed. 'Tell him he can take my tonsils out anytime he likes.'

'That would be difficult for him, would it not?'

'Because you want to keep him to yourself?'

'No. Because you had them taken out when you were...'

Before Kitty could say 'Eight,' Laura did.

'Talking of Dougal. Oh Laura, I'm just head over heels in love with him. And he has vowed to give up all of his adoring fans who keep throwing themselves at him.'

'Hope he keeps to that.'

Ignoring Laura's concern, Kitty asked, 'You and Mike... I think you're just as dotty about him as I am about Dougal.'

'You're right. Oh Kitty, don't say anything to anybody but...' Laura looked furtively about before pressing her fingers over her mouth and then uttering in a soft, hushed voice, 'We're thinking of getting married.' Laura panted with excitement as she added, 'And you, Kitty, will be my brides-maid.' Suddenly Laura was overcome with a look of dejection.

'What's wrong?'

'Oh, Kitty, we have to get married in the registry

137

office in Fire Brigade Street.'

'Why?'

'Because his dear manic mama thinks he is pitching himself into the gutter by going around with the sister of a murderer. And she also added that she had not sacrificed the way she had to let him train as a quantity surveyor so he could throw himself away on someone like me.'

To Kitty, Mrs Bailey's remarks were just so stupid they were laughable. 'Laura,' she tittered, 'I hope her insanity doesn't run in the family.'

'You can joke about it but she added insult to injury by suggesting that no *respectable* person would wish to come to our wedding.'

'Ignore her ... as far as I can see the snobby old bitch is not all there.'

Laura could only give a downcast shrug but before Kitty could go on further about Mrs Bailey, Laura guided her into the far corner of the Palais de Dance powder room.

'What's the matter now?'

Laura looked nervously about before she whispered, 'Eric's trial has been set for the first week in September. My mum is up the wall with worry.'

'So what can I do about that?'

'You? Nothing ... but Connie has been such a great help and comfort to my Mum I just want her to know, and that would be through you, that my Mum is going to need even more ... understanding now that September is not that far away.'

Kitty nodded. 'I know that Connie and your mum have ... well they have set up a support group for each other ... well that's if you could call going twice a week to the women's group with the

138

children a support.' Kitty giggled. 'I would have thought spending all that time with Rosebud, Billy and Jackie would be enough to have you certified and straitjacketed.' Growing serious, Kitty placed her hand on Laura's arm. 'Now as soon as you have the exact dates I will take some of my holidays so I am there with you and I will see that Aunty Kate watches the bairns so Connie can be with your mum.'

'But I thought that you said that your aunt and her husband were going to adopt?'

'They are but minding four children will be as easy as minding one.'

In the past Kate had always put her feet up after lunch. However, as soon as Hans left to go back to his shop, she found herself with three children needing looking after and entertaining.

She had just made up her mind to go over to Leith Links, and in particular to the swing park, when the outside door opened and she heard Connie call out, 'Nothing to worry about, Kate. It's just me, Nessie and the bairns. Thought we'd call in and welcome...'

By now, Connie and Nessie were in the living room and they were so stupefied by the sight of three children that they were stunned into silence.

Not wishing to embarrass Amos and Ben, Kate jovially said, 'Things didn't go quite as we planned. Amos,' at hearing his name Amos nodded towards Connie and Nessie, 'and Ben.' Ben now nodded. 'Well they are a twosome. What I mean is they don't go anywhere without each other. And we liked them both so much that we agreed to take them both.'

Connie and Nessie exchanged bewildered looks with each other but still they stayed mute because they were now staring at Aliza. Nessie was so shocked at the sight of the child that she moved in closer to Connie. Although it would appear that nothing registered with Aliza, the child did feel the reaction, perhaps even the revulsion, of the two women and she slowly backed away until the back wall impeded her further escape.

Trying to divert the women's attention away from Aliza, Kate brightly commented, 'I can see Billy and Jackie but where is Rosebud?'

It was obvious from Connie's hypnotic stilted reply that she was still trying to figure out why Aliza was in Kate's care. 'Rosebud.' She looked about. 'Oh she will be here shortly. She has just been dilly-dallying along since Miss Glen, you know the lady who runs the Post Office and shop, gave her a lollipop that should have been thrown out.'

'Aye, that's right, Miss Glen said Rosebud could have it even though we had no sweetie coupons left,' Nessie managed to add incoherently because she too was transfixed by Aliza.

Kate was just about to explain about Aliza when Rosebud tumbled in the door. As she picked herself up she looked about the room until her gaze landed on Aliza. Her mouth gaped and the lollipop, which was stuck to her tongue, just jutted from her mouth.

No one who was present in the room that day would ever be exactly clear as to what happened next. What they do know is that five-year-old Rosebud slowly, as if in a dream, walked over to Aliza. Aliza looked directly at Rosebud who took the lollipop from her mouth and, bending forward, she prized open Aliza's mouth and pushed the lollipop in. 'I don't know who you are. But somebody's been bad,' Rosebud now looked accusingly at the three women, 'very bad to you.' She now put her arms around Aliza but Aliza stayed rigid. Rocking Aliza from side to side she surprised everyone when she then pulled Aliza's head on to her chest and in a voice full of music she uttered, 'But you don't hae to worry nae mair because I'm going to be your best friend and I'll look after you.'

The three women would swear that it was as if Rosebud had touched Aliza with a magic wand – a wand that somehow brought some thawing to Aliza – some healing. They all stood saying nothing whilst Aliza very slowly lifted her right hand and stroked Rosebud's face. To those who witnessed this happening it was as if Aliza appeared to be making sure that Rosebud was real – that she was no mirage but a real living and breathing person. Rosebud responded by gently stroking Aliza's upturned face. The two girls were now oblivious to anyone else in the room and slowly they allowed their heads to entwine and all that could be heard were the quiet sobs of the two children. Kate, Connie and Nessie had to fight back the tears when they witnessed the two little girls who had never known of each other's existence until today but somehow they had already formed a bond.

It was nearly five when Nessie and Connie said

they would need to be getting themselves back up the road. Rosebud, of course, had begged to be allowed to stay with Aliza. No one raised an objection.

When Kate saw Connie and Nessie off at the door she said, 'Aliza can speak, she just chooses not to. I am trying to teach her English.'

Connie giggled before quipping, 'Well it seems to me that if anyone can get her to talk it will be Rosebud ... mind you, when she does get Aliza chatting you might be surprised at just how colourful her vocabulary is.'

For some reason Johnny arrived home from London in the early afternoon of the Friday. When he called, 'Hello there,' to Connie, who was in the kitchen, she jumped and the pot she had just finished scrubbing slipped from her hand and splashed back into the sink.

Glancing up at the kitchen clock as she dried her hands on her apron, Connie exclaimed, 'Oh Johnny, is there something up that you are home so early?'

Johnny shook his head. 'No. In fact everything down in London is going just the way I want it to.'

'That right?' replied Connie, pulling out a chair from under the table and sitting down.

'Aye, priority is being given to the Welfare State and the National Health Service bills.' Johnny cocked his head and Connie could see that he was happy, very happy about that.

This pleased her because she had been worried that Johnny, who had never been out of the

Lothians, would not fit in in London – how wrong she had been. He had even managed to get himself a small flat at a reasonable rent. This meant he could privately go over and over the material that had been discussed that day, or more importantly what was to be debated the following day. This was so important to Johnny, who felt that as he had only been educated to a lower standard he had to be able to hold his own with those who had enjoyed advanced schooling – some even up to university standards.

Johnny was now looking out of the kitchen into the living room where he could see his baby daughter Jackie asleep on the couch. He smiled as he noted that Connie had put a coat over her even though the day was warm.

'I can see the wee one,' he observed as he turned back to look at Connie, 'but where is Rosebud?'

Before she replied Connie strummed her fingers on the table. 'Look Johnny,' she hesitantly began.

'Nothing's happened to her?'

'No, but here,' Connie replied, 'you'd better take a seat because I've something to tell you about Kate and Hans.'

'They've been turned down for adopting a son because they are too old?'

Connie shook her head. For the next five minutes Johnny just sat mute. He could not believe what she was imparting to him. From time to time he nodded, shook his head, clapped his cheek and his mouth gaped.

When Connie had finished with her tale Johnny sat for a few minutes in silence. He was obviously trying to fathom all that Connie had told him.

Eventually he said, 'Now correct me if I am wrong but the two boys...'

'Amos and Ben,' Connie said in an effort to get him to realise that the young lads were going to be his nephews and deserved to be known by their names.

'Aye, Amos and Ben will have problems settling down but they will adapt to life in Leith because Kate and Hans have given them what they want and that is to be brought up together,' Johnny mused more to himself, 'and it's in their interest not to rock too many boats.' Connie nodded. 'But from what you tell me the wee lassie is ... how can I put it...?'

'No other way than to accept that she has witnessed such unimaginable horrors and been so maltreated that she might never recover well enough to make anything of her life.'

Johnny sort of played a tune by continually blowing out his lips and put, put, putting. When the putting stopped he scratched his head before muttering more to himself, 'Okay, say I accept that you're telling me the truth, without any embroidery, then how come she has taken to Rosebud?' He was for all intents and purposes looking and speaking to Connie but in reality he wasn't seeing her. His mind could focus on nothing other than how his truculent five year old daughter could get through to this poor bairn when no one else could. Eventually he mumbled, 'Connie, I know I'm not the brain of Britain but I'm not a dummy either and what I cannae fathom is how come our Rosebud is able to get this bairn to respond. After all, she's only five. What I am trying to say is, how can she possibly understand enough to be able to help ... what's the wee lassie's name again?'

'Aliza ... the wee soul is called Aliza ... and I think that when she was born she was so beautiful that her mother, who obviously loved her so much, gave her a lovely name to match the joy she had brought to her parents.'

'But...' Johnny drawled and Connie could see that he was still trying to get his head round what she had told him.

Rising slowly she went over and stood behind him and started to massage his rigid shoulders. 'Johnny,' she began as she tried to soothe him, 'don't be so hard on yourself. I didn't sleep well last night as I tried to sort it all out in my mind. See when Kitty came in for a cuppa, before I could make anything for the lassie I blurted out the whole story. Told her I did I just couldn't understand what had happened between Rosebud and Aliza.' Connie sighed. 'Kitty told me that Rosebud had not suffered anything like Aliza would have but she did have an understanding of what it felt like not to have your mother, your own mother, around you. Seems, Johnny, that as much as we have all tried ... our Rosebud too is damaged. Her tantrums and, okay, not so much now, her shocking behaviour is her rebelling against her being cheated out of being the baby all the family loved and, more importantly, having an adoring mother. Kitty, and what a clever, sensitive lassie you have there, also thinks that Rosebud and Aliza will become soulmates and lifelong friends.'

Johnny had come into the house so happy that

145

all his doubts about being able to be a good Member of Parliament were unfounded and he was bursting to tell his family he was more than making the grade. Now, as he reached up to his shoulders to still Connie's hands he felt that somehow he was to blame for Sandra dying and the torment Rosebud had endured. Gently he began to massage Connie's hands and he hoped that this action would convey to her just how much she meant to him now and he wished he could have spoken to her – said to her that he was sorry, so very sorry, about the unbearable grief she had felt about losing their baby.

Although she was loathe to break the spell between them Connie knew she must also tell him that Davy, his youngest son, had not handled Sandra's passing well. 'Johnny,' she began, 'there is another problem we have to sort. I think we have not realised how badly your Davy has felt about his mum and Jack's passing and Bobby disappearing out of his life...'

Turning to face Connie he gulped before uttering, 'What is wrong with Davy? He is the life and soul of the party.'

'That's the problem, he's drinking too much. So we have to face that and do something about it before it ruins his life.'

'Don't be daft. When does he ever overindulge?'

'Most nights,' she emphasised. 'And listen to me, Johnny lad, I demand that you do something about it ... not only for Davy's sake but I also do not wish our two wee girls to see him falling in the door unable to bite his fingers ... like he did last Tuesday.'

Saughton Hall Prison was no five-star hotel. It was like the Model Lodging House in Leith, a cold impersonal building for the housing of the vulnerable.

It took effort on Nessie's part to enter the jail where her son was detained. Today it was still August and the weather was exceptionally warm and yet she shivered as she felt the despair of not only her own son but of all the other inmates.

Waiting for Eric to come through the locked doors she looked about the hall. Mothers, like herself, wives and girlfriends all dutifully attending, all with false smiles pasted on their faces. She huffed as she thought that they all would rather be outside in the back greens watching their washings dry in the sun. Today, being here was even harder for Nessie. Usually Connie would be with her and she would chat away about this, that and nothing at all, just so long as it distracted her. However, Kate hadn't been able to look after Connie's bairns because she had to attend a meeting at the school.

Nessie thought that would be a difficult meeting because Kate and Hans thought that as Aliza was of school age they would have to enrol her. The term was due to start next week and Aliza was now speaking to everyone – but only through Rosebud. The problem now was that Rosebud was in the catchment area for Hermitage Park Primary School and Aliza for Leith Links Primary – this unfortunately meant that when Aliza started her schooling there would be no one there that she trusted to interpret for her.

The meeting with Miss Henderson, the infant mistress at Leith Links School, was more painful than Kate had thought it would be. The supercilious woman's voice booming off the wall suggesting that Aliza's difficulties were such that she would be better catered for at Clarebank School for the mentally handicapped children and therefore she should be enrolled there, truly upset Kate. Resisting the desire to slap the woman, Kate's response was to scream directly into her face, 'But Miss Henderson, what benefit would there be in sending Aliza there when she is not mentally retarded – I repeat not mentally retarded?'

Unfortunately, Miss Henderson, unaware of how much distress she was causing Kate, smiled sweetly before simpering, 'And you would not need to take her or collect her from Clarebank School. You see, as all their pupils are incapable of getting themselves to and from school they are escorted on a special bus.' Ignoring Kate's utter dismay Miss Henderson continued, 'And she would also not be subjected to the taunts and bullying of children who would not understand her ... let's say ... difficulties.'

Kate had never in her life known such uncontrollable anger rising up in her throat – rising so fast that she literally felt it choking her. Pushing back her chair she began to raise her right hand to slap Miss Henderson across the face. Luckily Hans, who should have attended with her but was delayed, had come in and unknown to Kate had witnessed Miss Henderson's behaviour. All Kate knew was that before her hand

148

was fully raised Hans had grabbed her elbow and very sweetly he bowed his head to Miss Henderson before saying, 'Thank you so much for your information and understanding.' Kate gasped and was about to challenge Hans and urge him to stand up to this demon of a teacher when quietly, but forcefully, he added, 'I am aware that you are just repeating what the authorities' guidelines state. However, before you retire there will have to be a whole new way of thinking about how schools teach children who are highly intelligent, as our daughter Aliza is, but do not learn in the conventional way. Now my wife and I bid you good day.'

Before Nessie could divert her thoughts away from thinking of Kate and Aliza and how they were getting on at the school meeting she was surprised when Laura came in to join her.

'I didn't hope to see you today. I mean you visited our Eric just two weeks ago.'

'I know, Mum, but as Connie couldn't chum you and lavish all that moral support on you I thought I'd better pitch up to keep you company.'

'Oh dear, Laura, see now that I know that the date for the start of the trial is Monday the 3rd of September, my stomach is just churning. Oh Laura, what if...'

'Mum, don't cross the bridges 'til you come to them. And talking of bridges here comes our Eric and if his facial expression is anything to go by it is just as well I'm here to...'

'Hold the coats,' Eric suggested to Laura as he pulled out a chair from the other side of the table so he could obey regulations and face his visitors.

Nessie tried not to let her apprehension show but she was unable to control the tremor in her voice when she said, 'Well, son, not long to go now until you get your trial out of the way.'

'Are you saying that I should be looking forward to getting a date for my hanging party?'

'Eric, for goodness sake, think about Mum. You are her son. She loves you. She is demented thinking about what will happen to you if things don't go well. Can't you see that she spends all her time thinking about what she can do to help you?' Eric remained stony faced. Laura then said, 'Do you know she has even written to the King and asked if there is anything he could do to help you?'

Eric's derisive laughter echoed about the hall. 'Wrote to bloody Georgie did she? Well if she hasn't had a reply yet I can tell her he will do sweet Fanny Adams. I was all right to go out and fight for him and country but now the war is over nobody cares about what happens to the lads, like me, that gave their all while...' He hesitated because he did not wish to say aloud that while he languished in a German Stalag, his wife ... the unfaithful bitch that he should not have killed because she was not worth swinging for, not worth him being denied access to his young son for.

Before Eric could go on, or Laura or Nessie could respond, the visitors' door opened and in skipped Kitty followed by a rather distinguished gentleman, but as he advanced into the hall it was evident that he had had some sort of operation to his left eye which had left a small, twisted, protruding scar that detracted from his otherwise handsome face.

Laura then blew out her lips in relief when Kitty literally danced towards the table. However, she did note that the man who appeared to be fascinated by Kitty slowly turned away and she was disappointed when it became evident that she was not being escorted by him. Nonetheless, when Kitty reached her friends, Eric's upper lip twisted as he snarled, 'Keeping company with bastards now, Kitty?'

Taken aback, Kitty shrugged and looked about the room before replying, 'I don't know what you're talking about, Eric.'

'That right? You waltz in here with Felix Martin, who was giving you the glad eye, and you say you don't know who he is.'

'I've already said, Eric, I don't know the man.' Kitty was beginning to bristle and she added, 'And as to him ... what did you say he was? And how would I know whether his parents were married or not?'

Eric chuckled. 'Aye, well it is true that his daddy couldnae stand by his mother because he already had a wife but when I say he is a bastard I'm not talking about his birth certificate.'

Knowing that Kitty was more than rather against people being labelled "illegitimate" and then spending their lives being ridiculed because their parents were not married, Laura quickly interrupted with, 'And how do you know the gentleman, Eric? I mean he looks rather professional and prosperous.'

'Oh he is all that. And I can see you and Kitty

151

are ready to toady to him and I hope after he persuades the judge that I should...' Eric slipped his hands under his neck and stretched it.

'Are you saying that he will be the one arguing the prosecution's case in your trial?'

'Aye, Mammy, and he takes delight in twisting everything that a witness says to him. See when my defence laddie ... what's his name again...?'

'Bill Gracie,' Laura confirmed for him.

'Aye, well when he heard that Felix Martin, and by the way his mammy gave him that fancy name in the hope it would detract from him being a...'

'Eric, you are upsetting Kitty by using that word.'

'Oh and we all know that you wouldn't be wanting darling Kitty upset, would you, Laura?' Laura did not respond but her deep breathing spoke volumes. 'But believe me he is,' Eric added, 'and a right one at that. Anyway back to Bill Gracie ... he says that getting Felix Martin as prosecutor was a double-edged sword for us.'

'In what way?'

'It is bad news for me because Kitty's pal will want to hang me out to dry. But if Bill Gracie can have it appear that he is able to hold his own against him then it will be of great benefit to his career.'

'And who said politics all take place in Westminster?' Kitty quipped.

Relief seeped into Kate as she sat facing Miss Cameron, the infant mistress of Hermitage Park School. She had explained about Aliza and her dependency on Rosebud who was enrolled at

Hermitage Park School and was due to start there on Monday week.

'Now let me get this straight,' Miss Cameron said nodding her head as she tried to take in all the information that Kate had imparted to her. 'The child did not speak to anyone at all when she was rescued, is that correct?'

Kate nodded. 'The first person that she responded to was my niece, Rosebud.'

In an effort to try to have Miss Cameron take Aliza into her school Kate started to speak so fast that Miss Cameron put up her hand to signal that she should slow down and repeat what she had just uttered.

Swallowing and breathing in deeply, Kate calmed herself. 'And I am not lying to you when I say Aliza is intelligent. In the few weeks that she has been interacting with Rosebud she has built a considerable vocabulary and can make herself understood.'

Miss Cameron nodded again.

'Can't you see,' Kate pleaded, 'that it would be so wrong to send her to a, let's say, special school, and have her prospects in life affected by such a wrong decision.'

'And the boys you have taken on?'

Kate gulped. 'My husband ... well I know schools have regulations and standards to keep ... but after our experience at Links Primary, who had no hesitation in accepting to enrol the boys, well he thinks that it may be better...' Kate was flustering. She firstly didn't wish to say pay for them to go to Leith Academy. She was sure that would have Miss Cameron thinking that they knew that Leith Academy would not accept Aliza because there was an entrance test to be passed which Aliza would fail. Secondly, she was aware that Miss Cameron, being a practising Christian, believed it was her duty to bend over backwards to assist needy children. Naturally, Kate therefore wished Aliza to be under Miss Cameron's guidance.

'I see,' Miss Cameron answered through pursed lips. 'Well if that is how your husband feels, and as it would appear that the natural fathers of the children are dead, why don't you try to have them schooled at George Heriot's? They would be awarded bursary status there.'

Miss Cameron's remarks caught Kate off guard. She had never considered that the boys would be considered for such a superior school on a bursary basis.

A few minutes passed before Kate heard Miss Cameron quietly drawl, 'Now, Mrs Busek, here is what I think should happen.' On hearing Miss Cameron speak Kate sat bolt upright and she almost shrieked with delight when Miss Cameron continued with, 'That is we should try, in this school, to accommodate the little girl you are fostering. However, if it becomes apparent that the child should not be educated in a mainstream school, and that she continues to only respond through your niece, then we would require to have her assessed as to what kind of establishment would be best able to cater for her ... special needs.' Kate immediately nodded her agreement. What was being suggested was more than she had dared hoped for.

The evening meal and the observations of the Jewish faith had just come to an end and the boys had gone upstairs to get themselves ready for bed when Kate said, 'Hans, you know that I had an appointment to see Miss Cameron up at Hermitage Park?'

Hans nodded. 'Yes. I know that. I also know that you did not wish to say anything about that in front of the boys but I am anxious to know how your meeting went.'

'Better, much better, than I hoped.'

'So I take it that Aliza will be going to Hermitage Park School.' Kate nodded. Hans sighed and as his fingers started to rhythmically strum the table Kate could see that he was much relieved. She knew that there were other things about the children that they had to discuss and she wished to get these over with before Johnny arrived with Aliza and Rosebud, so deliberately seeming as if it was of no consequence she said, 'You know, Hans, how you have said that you are going to make an appointment with the headmaster at Leith Academy?'

Hans quickly replied, 'Oh Kate, I meant to say to you that I have already made an appointment to see the headmaster about Amos and Ben being educated there.' He paused. 'And before you say anything I am well aware that we will have to pay fees to have them educated there. I have already enquired as to the cost and the fees seem to me to be very reasonable and, what is more important, they are affordable for us.'

Kate's broad grin indicated to Hans she was in

no way worried about the fees and he was surprised when she moved her chair up beside him so that they could chat in confidence.

Immediately Hans asked, 'Is there a problem?'

'No. But, Hans, have you ever heard of a George Heriot?' Hans shook his head. 'Well,' continued Kate, 'when he died in 1624 he was a very wealthy man. He was a goldsmith to trade but he was also a Member of Parliament, a financier to King James...'

'Is this a history lesson you're giving me?'

'No. Just be patient, Hans, and hear me out. In his will he left the bulk of his considerable fortune. Hans he left £23,625.10s and 3 pence a staggering sum at that time, to be used to build a hospital for the rearing and educating of "fatherless bairns" and that hospital became George Heriot's School.'

Looking bewildered Hans could only mutter, 'That was a very good thing for him to do. But why are you telling me all this when we have so much to do to get our three children settled in schools?'

'That's just it. The school still goes on and it is now one of the most superior schools in Edinburgh. If we wished to have Amos and Ben educated there we wouldn't be able afford the fees. But, Hans,' Kate could hardly control her excitement as she blubbered, 'they must adhere to the trust stipulations and so that today, right now I mean, they must provide places, bursary ... or whatever, so that fatherless children may enjoy a privileged education.'

For the next few minutes, whilst Hans was

digesting all that Kate was telling him, all that could be heard was the comforting ticking of Kate's father's granddaughter clock.

Eventually Hans said, 'If your facts are correct then we must see if Amos and Ben's circumstances would make them eligible for schooling there. Surely with what they have been through it would be in the spirit of George Heriot to compensate our boys for all they have lost and endured.'

Before Kate could reply, Johnny and the girls arrived.

Immediately the girls fled upstairs because they didn't want any of the adults changing their minds about them being allowed to sleep together in Aliza's bed.

'Cup of tea, Johnny?' Kate asked, rising to check if the teapot was still warm.

Johnny shook his head. 'No, I must be getting back home – lots of paperwork to attend to.' Johnny now looked about the room and Kate noticed that he grimaced before saying, 'But seeing we are on our own could I ask if there's any chance you could perhaps ... well come up with the rest of my share of this house ... not immediately but as soon as you can?'

Kate then looked quizzically at Johnny. 'But you have a fat salary now so you can't be hard up.'

'You're right, I'm no hard up, in fact I'm flush. It's just that I think I should be ... well as Mum used to say ... getting my own doorstep. And if I had the money from you and putting a bit by in the bank every month when I apply for a mortgage they'll be able to see by my bank book that I'm reliable and I'll get it.'

'Oh, I see – you're going to buy a house.'

Johnny nodded. 'Aye, and as Edinburgh Corporation have waiting lists as long as your arm it is only right that people who can afford to buy their own homes do so. By doing that it makes homes available for rent to those who can't afford to buy.'

'Right enough. And there are plenty of good houses about here that you would be able to afford.'

'Oh, I wouldn't be buying here.'

'You wouldn't?'

'No, Kate.' Johnny moved in closer to her before he confided, 'I'm hoping to go to the likes of Davidson's Mains.'

'Davidson's Mains!'

'Aye, you see I like this being down in Westminster and it would be in my best interest to be housed in the community that I'm representing.' Silence. 'Surely Kate, you can see that if I hope to get re-elected I have to do everything I can to make that happen.'

It took Kate quite an effort to stop herself from laughing. She just couldn't believe that her brother, Johnny, who up until now had always said that he would never buy a house, was suggesting he had changed his mind, but not only that, he was proposing to go to upmarket, Davidson's Mains. Well, she thought to herself, if this turn up was not her brother's "Road to Damascus" moment she didn't know what it was. After all, he had always maintained that he was a

158

Socialist through and through and purchasing private anything, he preached, was not for him.

Johnny proposing to buy a house was temporarily laid to rest when Hans said, 'Here, Johnny, what do you know about George Heriot's School?'

'It has a good name but it is fee paying.' Johnny sniffed and adopted his pious political face before adding, 'You and Kate know my views on it being wrong for any parent to be able to buy privilege for their children. Oh no,' he further sermonised, 'every child, from any walk of life, should be able to have good schooling. Superior education that should, and will, be provided by the state.'

Kate banged her hands on the table and her derisive laugh echoed around the room. 'Johnny,' she eventually hollered, 'listen to yourself. Here you are telling us that we are wrong to want Amos and Ben to go to Heriot's...'

Johnny's jaw gaped and his eyes bulged. 'You are thinking of sending them to Heriot's and yet you say I have to wait to get my inheritance!'

'We are thinking that way, Johnny. And as they are seen as "fatherless" they would get founder's places. But even if we were in a position to pay we would and, Johnny, before you accuse me of getting above myself again could I say to you that the minute you buy a house you have already stated that you wish to be different ... have privilege.'

'What do you mean?'

'Johnny, whenever you purchase a house you have asserted your right to privately provide your own housing. Not only that, when some people realise that they cannot afford the fees of private schools they then buy into districts where the

159

state schools, that their children will attend, are deemed to be superior.'

Johnny shook his head. 'Naw. Naw. I've always been proud to say where my home is and I will continue to do that.'

'That right?' Kate was chuckling again. 'Well could I ask you to think back, back to when Kitty was applying for jobs and her mother, your then wife Sandra, asked Mum and I if she could say that her family home was here and not in condemned Ferrier Street.'

# PART FIVE

## SEPTEMBER 1945

Back in June, when Eric was charged with Edna's murder, September had seemed a long way off. However, as Kitty strolled up Restalrig Road towards the bus stop, she thought so much had happened in that time. Last Monday when she was granted holiday leave for this week, she couldn't believe that this day of reckoning, this Monday the 3rd of September 1945, had now arrived.

Glancing up to the bus stop, which was situated just at the YMCA building, Kitty could see that Laura and her mother, Nessie, were already waiting for her. So just in case the bus was early she started to trot towards them. She had just crossed over Restalrig Crescent when she became aware that both Laura and her mother looked as if they had not slept a wink and not just last night but for a few nights.

Before Kitty could say anything Nessie grabbed for her hand and she muttered, 'It's so good of you to take your holidays so you could be with us. Oh, Kitty, my stomach is just rumbling with the nerves. I just wanted this day to come so we could get it all over with ... but see now it's here... Oh Kitty, I just ... no I won't be able to ... I mean what if...?'

Wrestling her hand free from Nessie's grip, Kitty

tried hard to think of something to release the terrible, unbearable stress that Nessie and Laura were enduring. Then to the surprise of Nessie and Laura she raised her left hand up to her cheek and as she patted it she said, 'Which day of the week does Nicol the coal man come?'

Nessie and Laura exchanged bewildered glances. Then Laura stared at Kitty whose hand was still on her cheek. 'Kitty,' Laura shrieked, 'oh, good heavens. Would you look at that, Mum, Kitty is sporting a three-diamond engagement ring!'

'Oh, Kitty,' exclaimed Nessie. 'I didnae ken you were courting seriously. I mean, I see Connie every day and she's never ever mentioned it.'

'My stepmother didn't know until last night and she was as surprised as you are.'

Before Laura could say anything the bus arrived and the three boarded it. Once they were seated, Laura, who was sitting with her mother in a seat in front of Kitty, chuckled, 'I am so pleased for you, Kitty. But I thought you were going to wait awhile?'

Still pushing out her hand so Laura and her mother could admire the ring, Kitty replied, 'You're right. We were going to wait. But, oh, Laura I just don't know what I am going to do. I mean I am so head over heels in love with him and now he is going to be leaving for Canada in just three weeks' time, I'm, well just absolutely...' Flashing the ring again Kitty continued, 'You see he wanted to be sure that I would go out to Canada as soon as I have qualified so that's why we got engaged. Mind you I won't be able to wear the ring in the hospital because we are not supposed to get engaged or even worse marry.'

'Why don't you just get married now … after all, you won't exactly need to work since he will be earning a doctor's pay?'

'No. I must finish my training.'

Laura could have continued the argument but she knew Kitty all too well. Oh yes, if Kitty's made her mind up then that is how things will be. What Laura did not understand was that if Kitty was so much in love, why could she not make the sacrifice that Dougal was asking her to?

By the time the bus had gone along York Place and was reaching the terminus in St Andrew's Square, Laura had grabbed hold of her mother's left hand that she was continually opening and shutting. 'It's all right, Mum. We are in plenty of time so we will just stroll up to the…'

'Think it would be best if we went up by the Bridges,' Kitty mused. 'What I mean is going up the Playfair Steps would be fine for us but…'

'You're right, Kitty.' Laura chuckled and cuddled in closer to her mum. 'And thanks to me wearing my new high-heeled shoes, not only are there too many of the Mound steps for you to climb but I too would be crippled by the time I got to the top.'

An uneasy silence had overtaken the three women by the time they got to the City Chambers in the High Street.

'We best cross here,' Laura said, 'the High Court is just behind the cathedral.'

'Could we no go up the way a bit and pass the front of St Giles'?'

'Why would you want to do that, Mum?'

'Well if it's open I could just nip in and say a prayer.'

'It won't be.'

'Then the best thing I can do is stand at the closed cathedral door and have a word with God.'

Laura and Kitty exchanged glances and just shrugged.

'Sure if God wants to hear me he won't be letting big doors get in his way,' Nessie pointed out to the doubting girls. When she finished her prayers she lifted her head and with a curt nod she indicated she was ready to go into the court.

As they walked Kitty observed, 'Know what has just dawned on me?'

'No.'

'Well Laura, this High Court is hidden from view from the High Street. It's as if it is hiding from prying eyes. It's in a wee world of its own.'

'Not so much of the wee,' Laura countered as she gave an involuntary shudder. 'I mean the height and grandeur of these buildings intimidates you.'

'What's that statue there?'

'That man on the horse, Mum?'

'Aye, looks a bit Roman like.'

Kitty laughed. 'He is dressed up like a Roman emperor, but it is a statue of Charles II and the pedestal the statue is mounted on is made from Craigleith stone.'

'You got any more information that will be of no use to us today?'

'No, Laura. Now as your mum is a witness she won't be allowed into the gallery to watch the whole trial. So I think we should go and ask what would be best to do.'

'Like what, Kitty?'

'Don't get so exasperated, Laura. We have to do what is best for your mum and that might be that they will allow you to stay with her and I will watch from the public gallery.'

While Laura was away making enquiries Kitty strolled with Nessie around the building. Firstly they walked about the grand hall and Nessie enquired of Kitty, 'They men in the long black robes that are walking about in twos, why are they whispering to each other?'

Emitting a soft laugh Kitty replied, 'They are the advocates, the top lawyers and what they are doing is tradition...'

'Tradition ... they look to me as if they're going to a fancy-dress party.'

'Forget the advocates, see here down at the bottom of the hall ... that stained-glass window depicts the enthronement of James V of Scotland ... you know he was Mary Queen of Scots' father.'

'But she cannae be the woman that's sitting at his feet because...'

Kitty tittered, 'No that's his mother, Queen Margaret.'

Nessie sighed. 'You know a lot about history, Kitty.'

'Yeah. At school it was one of my best subjects and one day our history teacher brought us up here and he told us all about the history of this building. Which reminds me...' Kitty grabbed Nessie's arm and steered her out of the hall and into the main corridor leading to the courts. 'See these two statues there.'

'They right ugly old things that are needing mended and cleaned up?'

'Possibly you're right but they are Justice and Mercy and that's what I hope we get in here for Eric.'

Before Kitty could explain anything further to Nessie, Laura returned. 'Good news. They will allow me to stay with Mum, but you, Kitty, will have to go into the public gallery. But the guy says he will put you in at the top of the queue.'

'Top of the queue?' queried Nessie.

'Aye, seems that Eric's trial is causing a stir.' Nessie looked abashed. 'That means, Mum, there are more people wanting to get in to hear it all than they can accommodate.'

Without another word to either Kitty or her mum, Laura tucked her hand under her mother's elbow and directed her in the direction of the witnesses' room.

Kitty then sauntered over to the head of the spectators' queue. To pass the time she thought back to that day when Mister Elliot had brought her class up here. It had been so exciting. Most of the children had never been up in Edinburgh Old Town and they were just so fascinated. She suppressed a chuckle when she remembered how Violet Jack had nearly fainted when Mr Elliot pointed out 'The Scottish Maiden' – the guillotine that had been used up until around 1710 to behead murderers, body snatchers and pirates. Whilst her classmates were looking agog at the machine Joe Gibson said, 'Mister Elliot, sir, did onybody ever live efter getting their heid chopped aff?' Mister Elliot's eyes glazed over, as they usually did when Joe asked a question, and Kitty was sure that up until the day all her classmates left school to start work, Mister Elliot had never ever answered one single question posed by Joe.

Sitting outside the infant mistress's office Connie continually kept rubbing her hands then patting down her hair. She just didn't know what this was all going to be about. Rosebud seemed so settled at school and Connie also thought that her colourful language was less blinding. She sighed as she conceded – well at home anyway.

Trying to calm her nerves Connie remembered that Rosebud was told by Miss Cameron that her mother must read the private letter in her school-bag but that it was nothing to worry about. Puffing, Connie thought that it was true that the letter said nothing worrying ... all it really said was that she was to come to school today to attend a meeting with Miss Cameron about Rosebud's education.

Connie was now nervously recalling how Johnny, when he was at home, was always emphasising that there must be no scandal attached to the family. Biting on her lip she could already see the newspaper front-page story: 'Labour politician for Wider Granton's five-year-old daughter expelled from Hermitage Park Infants' School for suggesting, in colourful language, that the infant mistress's parents had never been churched'.

Before Connie could let her fantasy go any further, the door opened and Miss Cameron invited her into her office.

Connie had just sat down when she blurted, 'Look Miss Cameron, if you have asked me in here to tell me that Rosebud is badly behaved, upsetting the class or can't keep up with her lessons could I ask that you take into consideration that...'

'Calm yourself, Mrs Anderson. I have asked you in here today because I would like your permission to have Rosebud moved into another class.'

'So she has been behaving badly? Look, her father can't have any scandal so if it means shifting her to another class and not throwing her out...'

'Mrs Anderson, this is a place of learning and we do not throw our pupils out. And even if we did that certainly would not apply to Rosebud. She is a very well behaved child and is exceptionally bright, but there is a problem.'

'Her swearing?'

'No. If she swears she does not do so in school. The problem is Aliza, and she too is settling in and doing well, but if she is to grow independent then she must be separated from Rosebud. It is also in the children's interest that they form positive relationships with other children.'

'Oh I see. They are too pally with each other and therefore don't play with the other bairns.'

'Precisely. Now what I propose is that as the April class is only three months ahead of the August one, I transfer Rosebud into that class. Now don't worry about that as she will soon catch up. So let's say that we move her from next week into Mrs Allen's class.'

'But if she is used to being in the top of the class won't it be a bit of a...' Connie was lost for the right words.

'No. I will give her a half hour extra tuition every day until she adjusts. Mrs Anderson, I am just trying to do my best for Aliza who will, or must, make the grade without Rosebud's assistance. What I am saying is that they need time apart so that both children are able to reach their full potential.'

Connie nodded her agreement.

'The last thing I wish to ask of you is that you do not mention our meeting and agreement to Mrs Busek until I have time to discuss the changes with her tomorrow.'

A hushed silence took over the convened Court Room Number One when the door opened and in came the judge, followed by a court official who hung the mace, the sign of the authority of the judge and court, up on the wall behind the judge's large, imposing chair.

As soon as the judge was seated, Eric, accompanied by two prison wardens, was brought up into the court. A lump grew in Kitty's throat when she looked at Eric, who appeared to her to be so isolated in his allotted space. She could not help herself from recalling the Eric of old when he had been a carefree teenager. Reluctantly, she admitted that he had always been a bit of a softie ... definitely his mother's son. In fact, Kitty had always wondered how efficient, clever, strong Laura was so very different from her mum and brother and as to her father, well all Kitty knew about him was he worked long hours, enjoyed his garden, fishing, and the only treat he ever had was a pint in the Lea Rig Bar on a Saturday night. These thoughts only served to make Kitty wonder what happened to Eric in the prisoner of war camps he was detained in for nearly five years. What did they do to him to turn one of nature's gentle creatures into the man who had brutally put an end to his wife's life?

The wigged and red-robed judge, bringing the court into session, put an end to Kitty's meanderings and her attention was now focused on the prosecuting advocate, Felix Martin, who really sounded quite unemotional in his opening statement which outlined the reasons why Eric had been charged with murder. It was then the turn of defence counsel, Bill Gracie, whom Laura thought was young but Kitty knew that between getting his degree from Edinburgh University and doing his two years' training, and four years actual practicing experience she reckoned he must be at least thirty. Kitty could see that Bill Gracie, dressed in his black flowing robes and white wig, looked the part but would he be an able adversary to the distinguished Felix Martin? After all, Felix Martin was not only at least five years his senior but was also a candidate for King's Counsel. This coveted title was only awarded to those who met the stringent qualifications.

By lunchtime all that had really happened was that both advocates had laid out their cases and what evidence they proposed in future to lay before the jury. Lunch for Kitty was a sandwich and a cup of tea in a small café in the High Street because the witnesses had other arrangements made for them. As soon as the afternoon proceedings were concluded Kitty met up with Laura and her mum. However, it was not until they were in the safety of Nessie's home, where they would not be overheard, that they started to discuss how they thought things had gone.

Nessie was the first to comment with, 'It's all so above my heid, so it is. And that court, it's so big and them all wearing they robes and wigs puts the frighteners on you, so it does. I mean what would the like of them know about folks like us?... Bet they never have slaved just to provide their crusts.' Nessie was now near to tears.

'I know what you mean, Mrs Stewart. And thankfully you weren't there to listen to that Felix Martin announce that he would prove beyond all reasonable doubt that Eric had, in a wicked and reckless way, murdered Edna. I just wanted to scream down to him that he didn't have the right to say that because he didn't know Eric ... didn't know the provocation he had suffered. As for Eric being truly wicked, if he was guilty of that why did he not put an end to...'

Laura quickly interjected. 'Calm it. This is just the first day and it looks to me that this trial is going to run for at least two weeks so we have to keep positive. Don't see it all...'

'Sorry for sounding off, Laura. It was not helpful. And did I hear right when you said that you thought the trial will last two weeks?'

'Yeah. Or so I was told.'

'In that case I think it would be better for me to get down on my hands and knees and beg Sister Doyle to let me come back to work this week and allow me to take next week off.'

171

Laura nodded. 'Yes, I would like you to be with me then because Mum will have given her evidence and we will all be able to sit in the public gallery together when the verdict is read out.'

Like Connie had been, Kate was just so uptight about her meeting with Miss Cameron. As she walked up Lochend Road towards the school she thought just how lucky they had been, firstly by getting both Amos and Ben into Heriot's. Mind you, after they had sat the entrance exam she and Hans had been surprised when the assistant head teacher had said that one of the boys was exceptionally gifted and his IQ was quite high. Hans and Kate, of course, assumed he was talking about Amos but then the tutor went on to say that even though Ben's English needed quite a bit of polishing this would in no way, because of his fortunate ability, handicap him. He had then gone on to say that Amos would probably struggle a bit at first but that he too would make the grade necessary for admission to George Heriot's School.

Kate was nearing the school gates when she admitted to herself that she and Hans had not expected the results that the tutor had given them. In Ben's case she wondered if he, to a much lesser degree, was suffering from the same post-traumatic stress that afflicted Aliza. If he was then, in time, she hoped he would recover and take advantage of the opportunities that were being afforded him.

Breathing in five deep breaths she then climbed the five steps into the school. 'Dear God,' she silently prayed, 'please let her tell me something positive about Aliza.' Kate, as any natural mother would, required that because in the short time she had assumed the role of mother to Amos, Ben and Aliza she had grown to love them. And now like any mother she wished the very best for them.

When Dougal, bleary eyed and yawning, answered the three o'clock call from the duty staff nurse in the men's medical ward, he was surprised when he ushered himself behind the screens to find the assisting nurse there was Kitty.

After attending to, and advising on, the treatment that he thought the very sick man should have he followed Kitty into the sluice where she had gone to empty a sick bowl.

'Here am I,' he laughed as he grabbed her around the waist and danced her about the room, 'thinking that you, who I am engaged to, had deserted me so that you could prop up Laura in the court.'

Before he could continue, Kitty wrestled herself free. 'The case is going to last at least a week, perhaps two, so I asked, and was granted permission, to take the rest of my annual leave next week when the verdict will come in.'

'Talking of the verdict, how do you think it will go?'

'The problem is that he insists he just intended to have a talk with Edna – to try and get things resolved for Billy, but he took his father's gutting knife with him.'

'Right enough he would have some job convincing a jury that he intended to go fishing, especially as he didn't take a rod.'

'You've got it in one. Which could result in him being sentenced to,' she gulped, 'hang ... but I'm sure that on appeal ... well you never know ... but the Prosecution's man is very able and sounds so convincing. To be truthful I think he is a person who has not known much happiness in his life and he is therefore ... indifferent to the suffering and problems of others.'

'Anyway back to us. Please tell me that you are about to make me the happiest man in Leith today.'

'And how could I do that?'

'By agreeing to marry me now and then we can both get on the ship bound for Canada and kid on we are honeymooning on a slooooow boat to China.'

'No. As I have said over and over again, if you love me you will allow me to finish my training. You know how much work I have put in so far and before my top dream was to be married to you, it was to become a state registered nurse.' Dougal huffed and puffed. Kitty slid her arm through his. 'But I will compromise and get to you just as soon as I have passed my final exams.'

Gently licking her cheek, Dougal whispered, 'Since you are in the mood to compromise I don't suppose you would consider spending one night of raging passion with me...'

Pulling herself free from him Kitty spluttered, 'I trust you are joking.'

Dougal shook his head. 'I would even bankrupt myself and pay for a night in the bridal suite of the Caledonian Hotel.'

Kitty had advanced to the door. 'Think you should spend your money on having a psychiatric assessment.'

The dulcet tones of Sister calling, 'Nurse Anderson,' had Kitty open the door and she fled back into the ward.

Amos and Ben, although settling down with Hans and Kate, still felt the need to escape upstairs after supper. Time just to be with each other seemed so necessary. What they discussed Kate never knew but she did hope that in time they would feel so comfortable with Hans, Aliza and her that they would start to think they were part of a family again.

The meeting with Miss Cameron brought the necessity for Amos and Ben to start to freely mix with other people right to the forefront of Kate's mind. 'Hans,' she tentatively began, 'the meeting I had with Miss Cameron...'

'A problem?'

'No dear, far from it. She was saying that Aliza, despite her lack of fluency in English, is coping quite well with her schoolwork.' Kate then tittered. 'Said you and I are doing a good job with her. But in class Aliza never answers without referring to Rosebud first so to help both children to develop as individuals, Rosebud is being put up into the April-intake class.'

Hans nodded to acknowledge he thought that would be a wise move.

'So we will see how things go with Aliza. But after talking to Miss Cameron I started to think that Amos and Ben, although to a much lesser degree, have a similar problem.' Hans nodded. 'So I was wondering what it is that we could do to have the boys do something individually.'

'You mean something that the other is not involved in?'

'Yes.'

'Well Amos likes to play the piano ... trouble is we could get him lessons but he would really need an instrument here at home so he could practise.'

Kate looked about the lounge. It had been built for family living but not for housing large pianos. 'Don't suppose an accordion would suffice?'

Hans chuckled. 'Hardly ... but as we own this house we could sell it...'

'Sell it,' exclaimed Kate. 'Oh no, that would be like insulting my parents. They worked so hard to buy this home.'

'Yes that's all true. But knowing your mum I think she would be so pleased to know that she had left us enough equity in this house so that we could move on.'

'But where would we go?'

'We will have to look about. At this present time we can't move out of the district because Aliza is settling in so well at Hermitage Park School. But we have to have a bigger house for us all to live comfortably together. And we could also pay Johnny from the proceeds we get from the sale of this house.'

'Just a minute, Hans, what kind of house do you think we could buy with what will be left?'

'Kate, I know that your parents did not think a mortgage was a good idea but that was in their day. Times are moving on.'

'Are you saying that debt is not something that is shameful? All my life I have avoided it. I have never even taken out a Leith Provident mutuality loan.'

'I am well aware of how thrifty you are. However nowadays it is quite acceptable for people to take on a loan to buy a house.'

'That may be true but I know that the banks only give you a loan provided you don't require one. And what collateral could we offer them?'

'We would not require any because the security is in my ability to make money. Kate, my dear, when they look at my shop's accounts they will give me a mortgage.' He hesitated. She could see he wished to say something that was proving difficult for him. Taking her right hand in his he then placed his left hand under her chin so that her face was lifted up and they were looking into each other's eyes. 'When we buy the house there will be the added bonus that I will be living in a house that I have helped to buy... Can't you see I need to provide for you and our...' he gulped before uttering, 'children. Kate, I have pride again and I accept that you restored me to being a man who wishes to be responsible for his family... Besides, I don't need to be a lodger any more.'

Time ticked by. Kate was in deep contemplation. Eventually Hans could see that even although she did not utter a word she was accepting that she would have to bow to what he wished. He knew that her compliance was not through weakness – indeed he felt there was no woman in Leith as strong as she was. However, his ace with her was that she loved him so much that, even if it was against her better judgement, she would always put his happiness and well-being first.

Kate agreeing to his plans to move house had Hans become quite animated and he chortled and rubbed his hands together as he said, 'So back to where we were, dear ... what do we have Ben get involved with that Amos would not wish to do?'

'No use in suggesting that he joins the school rugby club because he shies away from anything that involves rough and tumble.' Kate looked earnestly at the wall before she added, 'But he does like to exercise himself so how about we suggest to him that he joins the swimming club at the Victoria baths in Junction Place? That would also have him meet different children than those he goes to school with.'

'Hmmm,' replied Hans, 'I was thinking more like him learning something like ... chess.'

Kate rolled her eyes to the ceiling. She wished to retort that there were times that Hans seemed to forget that he was no longer living a privileged life in Warsaw. The truth was that he was now living in Leith, where most people had to manually earn their living. However, she accepted that Hans was wishing to do for Amos and Ben what he would have done for his own children so she softened the retort she wished to hurl at Hans to, 'But would that not rather limit the number of children he would be mixing with?'

Hans shrugged his shoulders. 'Fine, Kate, swimming it is for now.' She looked directly at him and he knew from her gaze that if it came to what she thought was best for the children she would not back down. Quietly he added, 'But if he ever states that he would like to join the chess club at school I am sure you will give him every encouragement to do so.'

The third day of the trial found Laura sitting in the public gallery. Her mother was due to give evidence today and as she could not accompany her into the witness box Laura felt that if her mother knew she was close by that would be of some support to her.

They had heard that on the second day, the witnesses who were questioned in the morning were from the ambulance staff, Doctor Lawson and the theatre sister. The afternoon session was taken up with the questioning of the police and, in particular, Detective Sergeant Mark Bolan. Laura knew that giving his testimony would have been so very difficult for Mark. So much so that he held on until the end of the day's proceedings so that he could shake Nessie by the hand and tell her that he was sorry about having to testify against Eric and that he was always thinking about her.

Laura at that time didn't know why but her thoughts lingered on Mark and her mother. They just seemed to have such a lovely, caring relationship. Was it more than that, she wondered. Quickly she dismissed that thought as she reminded herself that she and Kitty had such a bond ... a bond that had them stand by each other no matter what.

Her mother, taking the Bible in her right hand, and swearing to tell the truth and nothing but the truth, put an end to Laura's reflections, and she

179

flinched. She had to concede that what in fact was true and what her mother believed to be true could be and probably were two different things.

The prosecution's Felix Martin, led by showing Nessie the gutting knife that had been used to end Edna's life. Nessie nodded and confirmed that the knife was indeed that of her late husband's and on the day in question it had been taken by her son, Eric Stewart, from her house.

Felix Martin was just going on to question her further when Nessie turned and, looking directly at the judge she said, 'Yes, Eric did take the knife but it was for his own protection. You see he knew Edna would be with a man...'

The judge banged his gavel in six successive thuds. 'Madam, you may only answer the questions put to you. Not ones you think counsel should be asking.'

Nessie nodded. Her gaze then searched the public gallery and when she saw Laura she shouted up to her, 'Laura hen, they're trying to stitch him up. They don't understand that he was just going to...'

The gavel banged furiously again. 'Madam, if you continue to disrupt this hearing I will have you removed from the court and charged with...'

A howl of dissent went up from the spectators and drowned out the judge's words but Nessie had got the message and she nodded her head in acceptance of the judge's warning.

Felix Martin then asked Nessie, 'Were you aware that your son was going to confront his wife?'

Nessie paused before replying. 'Don't know about confront because I'm not sure what confront means. I just knew that he was going to meet up with her. Wanted to get things sorted out ... try and make a go of things again for wee Billy's sake. Wee Billy's their son.' More to herself she added, 'If I'd known it would end up like it did I would have stopped him.'

'When did you become aware that the knife was missing from your home?'

Sniffing, Nessie replied, 'When the police came and I searched the drawer and couldn't find it. I think he only meant...'

'The court is not interested in what you think. It only takes facts into consideration.' Nessie squirmed. She looked pleadingly at Felix Martin. But by his detached stance she realised that he was not interested in what had driven Eric to do what he was accused of, he was only concerned with getting a conviction.

Felix Martin was aware that Nessie was uncomfortable with his questioning. Without speaking to her any further he looked up to the judge, bowed his head and stated that his questioning of Nessie was over for now.

Immediately Bill Gracie rose to his feet and Nessie visibly relaxed. She was sure that Bill Gracie's questioning would be easier for her to deal with. And only she knew that he had primed her well.

'Now, Mrs Stewart,' he began. 'Could you perhaps give us an indication as to the mood your son was in on the day when his wife Edna Stewart met her death?'

Looking straight at Bill Gracie, Nessie began, 'To be truthful, since he came back from the war, it is so difficult to know how he is feeling.'

'Are you saying he was very different from the young man that left to serve his country?'

'Yes. The laddie that left was just a big softie. He was never any bother. An easy bairn to rear, he was. And even when Edna said she was having wee Billy he just couldnae get married to her quick enough. Oh he loved her and wee Billy. See when he came to tell me that he had been born he was so happy ... like a dog with two tails he was.'

Felix Martin coughed and looked up at the judge. The judge reacted by saying to Bill Gracie, 'Counsel, could you have your witness come back to your original question?' Bill nodded.

'Now, Mrs Stewart, we accept that the young man who came back from the war was very different...'

'Yes,' Nessie quickly interrupted, 'he was. You see he was treated like an animal and the things he saw and were done to him, honestly...'

The judge banged his gavel. He looked at the jury and said, 'The testimony of Mrs Stewart concerning her son's treatment in the war has no bearing on this case and you should disregard it.'

Bill smiled inwardly. The jury had now been given an instruction but no way could they forget Nessie's heartfelt testimony.

Nessie's ordeal, however, was not over because she then had to face Felix Martin again.

Pulling on the lapels of his black robe Felix Martin made a play of consulting his notes. 'Now, Mrs Stewart,' he began slowly and distinctly, 'can I take you back to Friday the 22nd June 1945?' She nodded her assent.

Laura exhaled long and huskily. *Take her back,* she thought, *no need to take her back – that is where she lives now. Oh yes, ever since that day, she has lived and relived it, always asking for reassurance that there was nothing she could have done differently that would have changed what happened.*

Felix Martin continued. 'Now you have stated that on that day you were of the opinion that your son, the accused Eric Stewart, had advised you that he intended to meet up with his estranged wife, Edna Stewart, at her mother, Judy Fox's, house in Primrose Street. The purpose of the meeting was to discuss reconciliation?' Nessie nodded. 'Earlier in the month your son had returned home from the war and found out that his wife had had a child that he believed that he had not fathered...'

'Well, since he was away for five years and the bairn is just a toddler what else could he think?'

'So would you say that he was rather put out...?'

'Well, I'm not in the same class as you but even in your class I would suggest that you would hardly be jumping for joy when you arrived home and the threesome family you thought you were had become four.'

Felix Martin made no comment on Nessie's observations. 'Now is it true that without consultation with his wife he asked you to remove his son William Stewart from her care and that you have been caring for him ever since?' Nessie nodded again. 'Was the little boy not .... let's say ... bewildered that a stranger, which is what his father would appear to him to be, had removed him and denied him the comfort that his loving mother lavished on him?'

'It's true that the wee laddie has been affected by all this. But it was the granny, Judy Fox, that was really caring for him and his wee half-sister...' Nessie hesitated. 'God please forgive me because it is bad to speak ill of the dead but Edna was wild when Eric got in tow with her but when the American soldiers arrived she just lost the place completely.' Nessie stopped and swallowed hard before adding, 'Mind you, Edna never ever really had the place. She, God rest her soul, didnae come from a family where she would have been told what was a sin and what was not.'

'I would put it to you that this is in your staunch Protestant opinion.'

Nessie's gaze now strayed over to the dock where her son was seated. She so wished to help him and she was going to say more about Edna but Eric had loved her, still did, and she decided not to add further to what she thought was wrong with Edna and her mother.

However, Felix Martin sensed Nessie's reluctance and very forcefully he said, 'Thank you for your vivid opinion on your daughter-in-law and her upbringing.' He rubbed his chin and pondered before adding, 'And you are asking this court to believe that when your son left your home on Friday the 22nd June 1945 to visit his wife, in what you consider a house of perhaps ill repute, that he had no reckless desire to avenge the embarrassing wrong that he thought his wife had done him?'

Laura could see that Nessie now realised she had made a mistake and had given Felix Martin some ammunition to use against Eric. She was just about to shout down that she wished Felix Martin to leave her mother alone when she was restrained by someone placing a hand over her arm.

'Kitty,' she whispered as tears surfaced. Kitty waved her hand to indicate that nothing should be said right now. All the comfort Kitty could give Laura was to link her arm through hers.

Nessie flustered then stuttered out, 'I didn't know that he had taken the knife with him. But it is wild in that street on a Friday night so I think he took it for protection.'

'Protection,' Felix said with an air of reflection, 'exactly from whom? Your son at five feet eight is four inches taller than what his wife was and his mother-in-law is, so they could hardly be described as menacing.'

'None of them,' Nessie shouted. 'He took it in case she was with a man again.'

'I accept that but that also means he intended to put an end to someone's life.'

'Noooooooo. What I meant to say was...'

Felix Martin bowed to the judge whilst saying, 'I am finished with this witness.'

When the court proceedings finished for the day Laura turned to Kitty. 'I thought you would not be back until next week. Tomorrow it's Judy Fox on the stand in the morning and Eric in the afternoon. Or that is the plan but they say it is flexible. Friday or Monday should see the summing up then the jury goes out and we wait...' Breathing in heavily through her nose Laura pressed her hand over her mouth before grabbing for Kitty's arm and whispering, 'I don't think I am strong enough to hear the verdict...'

'You are. And you will be there to help your mum no matter what the verdict is.'

Felix Martin made a big play of telling the jury how Judy Fox was a victim in this case – a grieving mother who had lost a dear and precious daughter. When he got down to the actual questioning of her, whom he had covertly coached, he said, 'Now I know how difficult it is for you to tell us, but in your own words, and in your own time, I wish you to tell us what happened in your home when the accused, Eric Stewart, burst into your house?'

'I remember the thudding on the outside door of my ground-floor home in Primrose Street. Then the door was kicked as Eric shouted, "I know you are in there so let me in." The door wasnae strong and it burst open and in he came. Edna was in the bedroom and he ran in there ... she was just no match for him... I saw the knife glinting before she jumped up from the bed and begged him to let him go... I mean, I mean, the knife go. She desperately wrestled with him and the next thing I knew there was blood, my wee lassie's life blood spurting all over the place, so much blood I knew she was done for.'

Eric jumped up and he pointed a finger at Judy but before he could speak he was restrained by both of his prison officers so he could only sink down dejected.

After that, Felix Martin only asked Judy about the calling of the ambulance and police and the police officer, Mark Bolan, calling late on to say that Edna had been pronounced dead.

Bill Gracie also started his questioning by offering Judy his condolences on her loss. He then adopted a rather soft approach, which Laura found annoying. 'Now,' he said, 'I just wish to say that it is acceptable to me that you answer my questions in your own words.' He allowed a brief pause. 'Your daughter, Edna Stewart, was she well on the 22nd June 1945?' Judy nodded. 'Not sick or tired?' Judy shook her head. 'Then why was she in bed so early, because in a statement that you gave to the police you said that she was a late bedder? I think you stated that she was never asleep before two o'clock in the morning.'

Judy looked over to Felix Martin, as if she was trying to get guidance from him, but his facial features remained impassive.

'She was in the bedroom by herself, getting titivated up to go out on the town, was all she was doing.'

'Mrs Fox, there is no easy way to put this but was your daughter working as a prostitute?'

Judy banged her hand down on the edge of the witness stand before she spat, 'She was not a prostitute!' Mellowing her tone she looked about the court. Kitty felt she was hoping to find someone who was sympathetic to her. 'She was young so she liked a good time,' she continued. 'What was wrong with that? She wasn't any different from anybody else her age. I mean it wasn't her fault that Eric got himself taken prisoner. Five years he was away. She thought he was dead. And when he came back he was so changed it would have been better if he had been killed.'

Bill Gracie did not challenge Judy on her statements. However, he did give a pensive look to his papers before saying, 'Now, Mrs Fox, who was the man lying on the bed with your daughter?'

'There was no man. That is just a lie that Eric concocted so he would get himself off with killing my Edna.'

'But you let it slip that Edna begged Eric to let whoever it was with her go. He must have been a right gentleman that he ran off and left Edna to face Eric who was chasing him with a knife.'

Judy Fox had endured a hard life and she was not the brightest star in the sky so she blundered on with, 'It wasn't like that.'

'No. Then how about you tell us how it was then?'

'My Edna,' Judy began with a voice full of emotion, 'oh aye, she was just so gorgeous and full of life that all the boys buzzed about her like bees around honey.' She paused. 'And she never sold herself cheap. She...' Judy realised she had now given too much away and she started to cry profusely.

Bill Gracie raised his hands to indicate that there was no point in going on with the witness. The judge nodded agreement and looking directly at a stone-faced Felix Martin he suggested it was a suitable time to adjourn for the day.

Once they were outside the court Laura turned to Kitty, and putting both her hands on Kitty's cheeks, she asked, 'How did you manage to get time off to come here? And more importantly how did you know I would need your support?'

Before Kitty could answer, Nessie came out of the court house and when she saw the girls she sprang over to them. 'I think I made a mess of it yesterday but see with what Judy has just said I think Eric might have a chance. What do you think?'

Kitty and Laura exchanged anxious looks with each other. Yes it was true that Judy would have made the jury think that there was a possibility that Eric had never intended to kill Edna when he entered that house. However, he had a knife, a knife he had deliberately taken with him because he had murder in his heart.

The following day it was Eric's turn to be grilled by Felix Martin. Nessie, Laura and Kitty, who had had just three hours' sleep after coming off night shift, sat silently in the public gallery. It was as if they couldn't bear to say to each other what they were thinking.

After being sworn in, Eric stood upright in the witness stand. He agreed with Felix Martin that he had taken the knife from his mother's house but he said that he had done so for his own defence because some of the men Edna associated with were villains. Felix Martin then put it to Eric that he had murdered Edna in a fit of jealousy.

Eric shook his head. 'Who knows?' he replied, staring ahead and seeing nothing. 'I don't think I did. You see I loved her, in spite of it all I loved her – still do. It was just that she had been brought up all wrong. She'd never been told that selling yourself to any man that wanted to buy was wrong ... and in Edna's case it was adultery.'

Felix Martin leaned forward, and looking at Eric but directing his voice to the jury he forcibly said, 'Mister Stewart, please just answer the questions that are put to you. Now is it true that you, with wicked recklessness, did stab your wife thus severing her carotid artery which resulted in her almost immediate death?'

Biting on his bottom lip Eric took time to compose himself before saying, 'I honestly don't know. All I know was I went down to Primrose Street to speak to her ... ask her to consider us getting on better. When I barged into the house, and I had to kick the door in, to get entry, all I can remember is that I heard Edna giggling. I thought she had a man with her in that bedroom and me her husband had never been in bed with her since I left for the war. Blinding rage consumed me. I wanted vengeance for all that I had suffered. Could nobody see my pain, my sense of betrayal? Everything after I opened the bedroom door and saw the man with her is a nightmare. I think I fished the knife from my pocket, I lunged for the man, then there was a scuffle... Judy says that I deliberately stabbed at Edna, no ... that just couldn't be ... if I hurt her it was an accident ... and who says I did it? When I realised Edna's blood was spurting from her...' Eric paused. 'I froze. And all I can remember after that was seeing the knife lying on the floor and I heard running footsteps out on the street.'

'So we are left with your story of what happened and Mrs Fox's and why would she lie?'

'Because that is all she has ever done where Edna was concerned. Oh aye, when Edna and I were first married and I would come home and find Edna wasn't there and when I asked where

190

she was her mother would always say, "She's away to the washhouse in Bonnington Road".' Eric gave a derisive chuckle. 'Edna away to the washhouse, well that's a big laugh because not only did she not know what a washhouse was for she didn't know how to wash. Believe me, it was my mother's job to run down to Primrose Street and collect all my wee Billy's dirty nappies and return them all freshly laundered.'

Felix then indicated with a nod to the judge that he was finished cross-examining Eric. Immediately, Bill Gracie got to his feet. However, before he could start questioning Eric the judge lifted his gavel and after banging it three times he asked both counsels to meet with him in his chambers. The macer then appeared and the mace was removed from the wall thus signalling that the judge was not in court.

Laura grabbed her mother's arm. 'Mum, what does this mean?' She then turned to Kitty. 'Do you know why they have gone away to have a discussion?'

'No. But what I do know is that there is something wrong ... very wrong. I've been watching the judge. Don't be fooled by the way he seemed to be unaware of all that was going on and a bit disinterested. Now yesterday when Judy gave her testimony, he became quite animated. What I am trying to say is that there was something about Judy's testimony that caused a change in him. And today from the start of the proceedings I noticed that he seemed to be completely engrossed with what Eric had to say.' Kitty paused. She did not wish to upset Laura and Nessie but

191

she had to prepare them for any change in the proceedings. 'I'm afraid we have to prepare ourselves. Whatever the judge says when he comes back into court please, please, do not overreact.'

'But what exactly has changed, Kitty?'

'I really don't know, Laura. But what I think is that the judge isn't at ease with what he has learned over the last two days.'

'Are you saying that he might abandon this trial and set a date for a new one with a different jury?'

Kitty did not reply but she pursed her lips in an effort to control her panic. She just had to keep calm because she did have some knowledge of the law and of court proceedings. To be truthful, she sincerely wished she had not become aware that a problem had arisen. But what was it? All she knew for sure was that the judge was not happy about something. She bent her head as she tried to remember everything that Judy and Eric had said. All she could conclude from going over their testimonies was that if she had been completely unbiased she would not have had a clear picture of what exactly had taken place the night Edna was killed.

An agonising forty-five minutes passed so slowly that it seemed to Kitty and Laura that it was more like three hours. At one time Nessie, Laura and Kitty would be huddled together to support each other then they would individually lean forward, willing the door to open again and the judge and advocates to return. At one point Nessie tried to catch Eric's eye. But since he was escorted back to the dock he sank down on his allotted chair and, holding his head in his hands, he rocked backwards and forwards in utter despair. Giving his testimony had brought all of the horror of that fateful night back. He tried ever so hard to push everything about Edna, and the way that she had been killed, deep down into his subconscious. It had also brought back the resentment of the way she had made such a fool of him, humiliated him, just like when he had been taken prisoner and all his rights as a human being were stripped from him.

When the two learned counsels re-entered the chamber followed by the judge and the macer, who rehung the mace on the wall, Kitty tried to gauge by their faces if they were pleased or put out. Bill Gracie, she thought, had a spring in his step. But when she looked at Felix Martin she couldn't fathom how he was feeling because neither his facial features nor his positive bearing gave any indication as to how his case had been affected by what had gone on in the judge's chambers.

Once the judge was reseated he banged his gavel three times. Kitty wondered why because as soon as he came back in to preside over the trial a hush had descended on the court – a silence that was quite eerie. All of them wanted to know what was amiss and yet some, like Kitty and Lorna, were terrified that they were going to have their worst fears confirmed.

The judge then took his time to start to address the jury. Slowly and deliberately he began with, 'After careful and deliberate consideration of the testimonies I have heard in this case I am of the opinion that the defendant's charge of murder should be reduced to that of manslaughter. I came to this decision after giving full and thorough examination of the facts.'

Loud cheering erupted around the chamber. Men who had been in the war and who had known what it was like to witness man's inhumanity to man and who would for the rest of their lives be changed by that, had dutifully attended the trial every day, and were relieved by the judge's decision.

Kitty slumped forward and her sobs were heart-rending. Laura's face was buried in her mother's neck. Nessie kept saying, 'But what does this mean. Is he free or what?'

Eventually Kitty stopped crying and she held Nessie's hand in hers as she said, 'The reducing of the charge from murder to manslaughter means no matter what the jury decide, that is whether they say, guilty, not guilty or not proven, your Eric will not be hanged. Do you hear me, Mrs Stewart, it doesn't matter now what happens, your son will not be hanged.'

Nessie turned to Laura. Laura, although choked with tears, managed to mumble, 'See, Mum, your prayers have been answered. You made me so frightened when you kept on saying that if our Eric ended up losing his life ... losing his life in such a brutal way that you would not have been able to go on. Now, Mum, I promise you, you will live long enough to see him a free man again.'

By banging his gavel, the judge eventually managed to impose his rule over the court again and once all the hubbub had died down he said,

'The proceedings of the court are over for today. Tomorrow both counsels will give their closing statements and I will then address the jury and go over points of law.' He then stood up, bowed to counsel, and exited the Chamber.

The agog public then took their time to vacate the public gallery. This was because most of the spectators appeared to have become quite animated after hearing of the change of the charge.

When Laura, Kitty and Nessie managed to fight their way through the dawdling throng they pressed on until they reached the front of St Giles' Cathedral where they huddled together. 'Oh, Laura,' Nessie managed to stutter, 'tell me again what it all means.'

'Just Mum, as Kitty said, that being charged with manslaughter is not a hanging offence...'

Before she could listen to what else Laura was saying to her mother, Kitty looked up and there passing on the far side of the road was Felix Martin. Immediately she recalled that when the judge made his life-changing statement for Eric, she had thought that this must be a severe disappointment for the Procurator Fiscal's office, and in particular Felix Martin, who, after all, had had their conclusions as to what Eric was charged with not only challenged, but set aside.

Kitty thought about how she would have felt and she wondered if Felix Martin would react as she would. It was always painful to her when in the hospital she was told that she had not quite got things right.

Without warning she sprinted over the cobbles and just as Felix was about to cross over the High

Street and past the Sheriff Court she caught up with him and pulled on his coat sleeve. 'Mister Martin,' she managed to mumble when he turned to face her. 'I know I have no right to speak to you.'

'You haven't?'

'But I just wished to thank you for allowing the change of charge.' She babbled on, offering her right hand to Felix which at first he seemed reluctant to shake, but then when he deigned to look at her he could not help but notice how the late afternoon sun lit up the highlights in her platinum blonde hair, which fell down onto her shoulders in deep natural waves. Although her hair was lovely and he was also captivated by her striking moistened green eyes, there was just something so enchanting about her. He then found it impossible to say to her that the change was completely outwith his control. And it was also quite out of order for her to speak to him about the case which had still to reach its conclusion.

'So you are Eric Stewart's sister?' was all he uttered. This mistaken identity was due to the fact that when the public gallery furore had begun he had looked up and he had seen that Kitty was completely overcome by the decision.

'No. I am no relation to Eric. I am his sister Laura's best friend and indeed I am also a friend of all of the Stewarts.'

Still holding her hand firmly in his grip he replied, 'I see. Now I do not wish to appear rude or abrasive but it is quite out of order for you to speak to me as I am *still* officially involved in the case.'

196

Kitty flinched back. She had made a mistake. Instinctively, as if she was trying to somehow rewind the last few minutes and not approach him, her left hand shot up to cover her mouth.

He didn't know why but his eyes riveted on the three-diamond engagement ring that, like her hair, caught the rays of the brilliant late afternoon sun and sparkled. Somehow it seemed to taunt him. This perplexed him, a feeling that was almost alien to him. But why was this slip of a girl, perhaps ten to fifteen years younger than he was, enchanting him? Letting go of her hand he regretted that he had spent his youth studying to get where he was today. He knew there were reasons for that but at thirty-five he found himself, for the first time in his life, lamenting that he had never known the excitement and ecstasy of young love.

When the court reconvened the following day both advocates expertly summarised why there should be a full examination of the facts in this case. Felix Martin went on to give the reason why the Procurator Fiscal had felt that there was a case to answer and why therefore Eric Stewart had been charged with causing the death of his wife, Edna Stewart. His final observation was that there could be no other verdict than guilty as charged. Bill Gracie's statement was naturally on why he was defending Eric Stewart against the charges laid on him. Kitty felt he was very persuasive when he pointed out that the case made against Eric was only tenuous, or to put it in another way, at best halfway plausible. His final remark was that there was no positive proof of Eric's guilt.

Before the fifteen-member jury, which was made up of eight men and seven women, retired to consider their verdict, the judge very ably summarised the main points in the case that required their attention and also the pertinent points of law.

However, those in the public gallery, although pleased that the trial was reaching a conclusion, felt that after the dramatic changes of the day before, the morning proceedings were an anticlimax and they were now anxious to hear the jury's decision.

The dilemma facing Nessie, Laura and Kitty was how long the jury would be in giving its verdict.

'What do you think we should do?' Laura asked of Kitty when they got outside.

'Well, they could reach their conclusion quite quickly and it will all be over this afternoon, which means we will be called back today. On the other hand they could take days.'

'Don't know what to do?' Laura said, more to herself than Kitty

'That right, Laura? Well, I do so let's have a long, leisurely lunch because there is no way we are going to leave here until court closing time.'

'I think you're right, Kitty. I am just dying for a cup of tea,' was Nessie's response.

It was three twenty when the jury sent out word to the judge that it had reached its verdict.

Kitty bit on her hand. Not good news because to reach their conclusion so quickly they must have a unanimous verdict and that could only be arrived at if all were of the same opinion ... but then she conceded it was too much to expect an eight to seven majority. She shook her head. What she thought to be true was, and she couldn't say this to Laura, that it was a complex case and in the final minutes of Edna's life there were only Judy and Eric left in the room.

The judge asked the foreman of the jury if they had indeed reached their verdict. He replied, 'Yes,' and the paper stating the decision was then handed to the judge. Whilst reading the paper the judge remained impassive. He then turned his attention to Eric whom he asked to stand whilst he delivered the jury's verdict. 'Eric Stewart,' he began, 'you have been found guilty of the manslaughter of your wife, Edna Stewart.'

Laura grabbed on to her mother and encircling her with her arms she murmured, 'Mum, we must be strong, hold our heads up, if not for our own sake, then Eric's.'

It was at that time that Felix Martin glanced up at the public gallery and he was unnerved when he witnessed distraught Kitty being comforted by a rather handsome and very caring young man. What he didn't know was that the young man was Mike Bailey, Laura's fiancé.

After his announcement of the guilty verdict the judge allowed a short interval for the court to settle down. Banging the gavel he indicated that he had more to say. 'It is now nearly court finishing time so I will not announce the sentence that I propose to pass on Eric Stewart until Monday next, the 10th of September 1945.'

As was to be expected the court room was full.

The trial had caused a great deal of interest – not only public interest but with the press, who were having a field day.

Nessie, Laura, Kitty and Mike were all seated in the front row and what was not evident to those in the main part of the chamber was that all four had linked hands.

The suitably robed and wigged judge entered, as per usual followed by the macer. He made a few opening remarks, which included his thanks to the jury before asking Eric to stand.

Nessie looked at her son and her heart fluttered. He looked so much older than his years and it was evident that he had not slept well. Rising to his feet she felt that all life and hope had been sucked from him. She knew he was facing a further curtailment of his liberty and that must be so hard for him to endure, especially as he wished to play a large and meaningful part in his son's life.

The judge began by saying, 'On reaching my decision as to the punishment I should pass on you, I had to take into consideration the amount of provocation that you may have endured. It is my considered opinion that there was substantial provocation and I therefore sentence you to six years' imprisonment.'

Laura began to slowly clap her hands and the rest of the spectators joined in.

Nessie turned to Kitty. 'What does this all mean?' Pulling Nessie into a tight embrace Kitty whispered, 'It means, my dear, that in four years, or less, your Eric will be a free man ... a free man, do you hear, and still young enough to start his life anew.'

# PART SIX

## MAY 1947

'You're half an hour late, Staff Nurse Anderson.'

Kitty looked down at the new watch that was pinned on to her uniform. 'Yes, you are quite right, Staff Nurse Keane,' she snorted, 'but you see the new intake of probationers do not, and never will, meet the exacting standards of nurses who have previously been trained in this superior hospital.'

Both young women then collapsed down on Kitty's bed as their uncontrolled laughter echoed around the room. 'You know, Dotty,' gasped Kitty when her hilarity began to peter out, 'we have now been practising staff nurses for three weeks and I still can't believe it.'

'It was me actually passing my final exams that still has me wondering if I am dreaming,' Dotty quipped with a shake of her head.

Chuckling, Kitty mused, 'Yeah. It was some three years but we made it, girl. And now Matron has accepted my notice, mark you in a voice that would have frozen the fires of hell.'

'That bad was it?'

'Bad? Let me put it this way, I think the word will be put out around the hospital that no one should dare speak to me ... a woman who has disgraced her profession by putting her own

201

happiness in front of fulfilling the binding contract that she made with this hospital three years ago.'

'How much notice are you to serve?'

'The obligatory one month. So that is just three weeks because the last week I am taking as my holiday entitlement.'

Dotty ran her tongue around her mouth. 'Have you written to Doctor Gorgeous and told him?'

Kitty looked down at her watch again, the gold timepiece that her Aunt Kate had given her as a present when she told her that not only had she passed her final exams but she was also dux of the class. In a half dreamlike state she then simpered, 'My darling man should be opening my letter right now. And know something, Dotty ... every week since he left we have exchanged letters. His were always so upbeat. I know you won't believe me but even although he is five years older than I am, he has never lost the recklessness of his madcap teenage years.'

'Lucky you.'

Both young women were now sitting on the edge of Kitty's bed and Kitty leaned sideways so she could cover Dotty's hand with hers. 'You're on holiday next week.' She hesitated. 'Is it not about time you went back to Ireland to see your folks ... to tell them that you made it?'

Dotty didn't answer immediately as the ceiling seemed to be holding her full attention. 'Oh Kitty, I would love to go back but I just don't want to be reminded about how awful my life was there. You know it was a teacher, a nun, at the school I attended who told me that I had potential and if I did not leave ... my family would pull me down.'

Three years it had taken Dotty to fully open up to Kitty. Kitty was now very fond of Dotty so she decided not to comment on anything that Dotty was saying until she had finished. 'You see, Kitty,' Dotty went on, 'my father is a drunkard and my mother took refuge in her religion. That meant she decided that none of her children would become a waster like my dad so to make sure we didn't she beat the hell out of us. We lived in squalor and ... well, I ran away. As I was leaving, that nun I told you about pressed my bus and ferry fare into my hand.'

'So your family might not deserve to know how well you have done but how about that nun? Come on, does she not deserve to know that you made it? Believe me, telling her will make her day.'

Dotty nodded. 'Aye, maybe you're right and as I will have our first month's pay in my pocket I can treat Sister Angelic to afternoon tea in a café.'

Kitty's mind now seemed to be running on wheels and she stood up and looked directly at Dotty before saying, 'Dotty, I have a favour to ask.'

'Ask away.'

'You know how I visit Laura's brother Eric every week in Saughton prison, well I was wondering if you would go and see him when I go?'

'Of course I'll visit the laddie. Especially since he has now lost his mother. By the way, how is Laura coping with her mum's passing? All too sudden and unexpected, so it was.'

'She writes that she is fine. Says she under-stands that all that had gone on with Eric had knocked the stuffing out of her mother and shortened her life. Pity Mrs Stewart never saw

Eric released but she did know that he intends to make a life for himself and Billy when he gets out. Oh, here, Dotty did I tell you he's been doing carpentry?'

Dotty shook her head. Kitty continued: 'Loves working with his hands ... creating things. Honestly, you should just see the beautiful wooden garden benches and stools he makes. They're so good that the prison has put them on sale to the public.' Kitty paused. 'I just know, Dotty, I really do, that when he gets released he will keep his promise to his mum and not go after Judy Fox for revenge.' Kitty then became pensive and Dotty didn't interrupt. Eventually Kitty drawled, 'It is just such a pity that Mrs Stewart's only regret was that she never did pick up the courage to visit Judy and say that she was so very, very sorry about what happened to Edna.'

'Talking of Judy Fox, what happened to the wee girl?'

'Adopted she was by a couple who were emigrating to Australia ... you know, on the ten-pound passage thing. I believe they are a lovely couple and they regretted that they couldn't have any children themselves so they adopted Ella. And when they arrived down under ... well nobody knew that the wee lassie wasn't theirs.' Kitty paused. 'I think the wee girl will have a nicer life there than she would have had here ... poor Judy was just not up to rearing her granddaughter.'

Glancing down to check the time again Kitty said, 'Look we're wasting our afternoon off. How would you like to come with me to visit Connie and the girls?'

It was true that Johnny wished to move house and he thought that he would like to buy in the Davidson's Mains area of the constituency he served. Connie, however, had pointed out to him, in no uncertain manner, that as he was away five days of the week and she was at home seven, Davidson's Mains was not an option that would suit her.

She did, however, agree that there was a dearth of Edinburgh Corporation housing for rent and needy people with children were therefore unable to be allocated suitable homes. This being the case, and as she and Johnny could afford a mortgage, they should be buying their own. Old Jock, Johnny's lifetime mate, thought that was all very well just as long as Johnny didn't begin to think, like some of his peers in the House of Commons, that he was a 'cut above' those he was representing.

It had been a difficult time deciding where they would look for a house. Both Connie and Johnny had to do what is usual in such a situation and compromise – more so in Johnny's case – and they now resided in a three-bedroomed terraced villa opposite the playing fields at Goldenacre. The bonus for Johnny was that his home was now on the direct route to his constituency and Connie was delighted that there was a bus stop just outside her door where the buses very quickly ran her back to Leith.

Ferry Road being a main road meant that unlike Restalrig Road, the front door was always kept locked. So when Kitty and Dotty arrived to visit,

Kitty had to ring the doorbell. When Connie did eventually open the door the first thing she said was, 'Now look here, I'm busy and I just don't have time to be entertaining Jehovah's Witnesses.'

'Is that so?' retorted Kitty. 'Well I do hope that doesn't mean that there is no hope of two newly qualified staff nurses getting their feet over the doorstep and a cup of tea.'

Connie stood back and signalled by waving her hand that the two young women were welcome.

'Nice house you've got here,' remarked Dotty after Connie had ushered then into the spacious living room. Connie sighed.

'You must like staying here,' Dotty enthused.

'It's okay but I do miss my old neighbours who were always popping in.' Connie huffed before adding, 'Two things for sure ... first is that you could die here and naebody would ken and second is that you could bet your bottom dollar that no one will ever rap on your door and ask for the loan of a cup of sugar.'

'That simply isn't true, Connie. Look at the help Miss Doig gives you.'

'Who's Miss Doig?'

'She's a teacher at Hermitage Park School. She stays round the corner in Clark Road and every morning, Dotty, she collects Rosebud and takes her to school and every afternoon she delivers her back.'

'Why doesn't Rosebud go to the local school?'

'She will be when the new school year starts in August,' Connie replied, continually nodding her head in confirmation, 'but you see, Dotty, when we first came here Kate's lassie, Aliza ... well the wee soul just wasn't ready to be without Rose-bud.'

'And she's doing okay now?'

'Oh aye, she's fairly come on.' Connie leaned in to take Dotty into her confidence. 'Last week she called Kate ... Mummy!'

Kitty smiled because that happening had pleased her too. With delight she remembered how Kate was so over the moon that she had felt it necessary to tell her five times within two hours.

'Look, Connie,' Kitty began, 'we are back on duty in a couple hours so when are you going to get around to giving us some tea and toast?'

It wasn't just the ringing of the doorbell that startled Kate it was also the quick, loud rapping. 'Amos, see who that is,' she commanded as she began to clear the tea table.

As was his custom now, Hans took nothing to do with clearing up the supper dishes and he was starting to go through to the lounge when he heard Amos speaking to someone and then the door close.

Hans just humphed thinking that Amos had dismissed some door-to-door salesman but when Amos arrived back in the hall he was not alone. Not only was he not alone but he was obviously visibly upset. 'Papa Hans,' he stammered, 'this young gentleman says he must speak with you.'

By now Kate had joined the three in the hall and as she looked at the young man she experienced a feeling of panic overcoming her and instinctively she fell back against the wall for support.

The appearance of the young man also caused the normally composed Hans to turn ashen, and as he extended his right hand, the stranger said, 'I am...'

'I know who you are,' Hans replied before the young man could finish his sentence. 'You see, your arrival is not unexpected. I have known from the start that you or someone like you turning up was more than a possibility. Now I think we should all go through to the lounge and sit down.'

The young man proceeded into the lounge first because Hans had hung back to assist Kate. 'It's all right, dear,' he whispered as he took her hand. 'Just you sit and listen whilst I speak with...' It was then that Hans became aware that Amos was still in the hall and very quietly Hans said to him, 'Say nothing just now. In fact come into the lounge whilst we find out *exactly why* young Mister Sisken has come.'

Once they were seated, Hans and Mister Sisken in the armchairs and Kate and Amos on the settee, Hans raised his hands to indicate to Mister Sisken that he should advise him of the reason for his visit.

'Firstly,' Mister Sisken began slowly, 'I apologise for coming so late in the day. But the last address that I was given for you was Parkvale Place. Unfortunately I had to wait until the new owners returned from work so that I could ask them if they knew where you were now residing. They were happy to advise me that you had bought this house.'

Hans, Kate and Amos all nodded. The selling of

Parkvale and their purchase of this end-terraced six-apartment villa in East Restalrig Terrace had been done in March last year. Hans, to relieve his stress, smiled to himself when he remembered how Kate had teased him by saying, 'Now before I start house hunting am I right in thinking that we are looking for a house that not only has a lounge large enough to house a piano, a separate dining room, located in the catchment area of Hermitage Park School for the convenience of Aliza, but most importantly, it has to be within walking distance of your shop?'

Drawing the long uneasy silence that had descended on the room to a close Hans linked his hands together before looking directly at the handsome young man and saying, 'You are aware that I know who you are, Mister Sisken. The family resemblance is quite remarkable.'

'You are correct and my name is David Sisken. My parents had five children. Only two survived … myself, the eldest of the family, and Benjamin, the youngest.'

'You are sure all the others are…'

'Yes, I have meticulously checked the records. The Germans are very good at administration and everyone who passed through their hands and what became of them was recorded.'

'Is it not true some records were destroyed?' Kate asked.

'Yes. But the ones that concerned my family were not.'

'So?'

'Well Mister Busek,' David looked about the room and when his eyes rested on Amos he seemed puzzled. 'I am here to take on the responsibility for my younger brother, Benjamin.' Pointing at Amos he said, 'But I do not recognise him.'

'That is because he is not your brother. David, may I introduce you to your brother's friend, Amos Kramer.' Amos got up and went over to David and shook his hand.

'I should explain that Ben – we call Benjamin what he wishes to be known as and that is Ben – is over in the Links playing tennis with some friends.' Hans had now got up and, placing a fatherly arm around Amos, he continued, 'Amos here prefers to play the piano.' David nodded. 'Now, Amos, would you just run down to the Links and ask Ben to come home?'

After Amos had left Hans said, 'Now, David, what are your intentions where Ben is concerned?'

'He is all that remains of my family and I intend, as I am duty bound, to look after him.'

'Does that mean that you intend to remove him from our guardianship?'

'Yes. And I do not have to point out to you that I have every right to do so.'

'Does Ben have no say in this?'

'Mr Busek, when you agreed to foster Benjamin it was on the understanding that should any family relative turn up then that relative had the right to remove Benjamin from your care.' David paused and seemed to ponder before adding, 'You and I are of the same faith so you know how important it is for families to be together.'

Defeated, Hans nodded.

Kate, unlike Hans, was not hampered by any religious obligations and she quietly, yet firmly, asked, 'And when did you last see Ben?'

'It was in 1941,' David answered quickly. 'That was when our family required to go into hiding. Good people sheltered us. Unfortunately in the four years that followed we were all *betrayed.*'

The emphasis that David put on the word 'betrayed' and his now heavy and laboured breathing made Kate realise that David was also a much damaged young man. She also realised that David and so many of the survivors like him would fight to their last breath to ensure that nothing like the Holocaust would ever happen to the Jewish people again.

'It has taken me from my release in 1945 until today to find Benjamin, my only surviving sibling.' David stopped. His head shook from side to side before he added emphatically, 'And now I have found him he and I will go to Israel and meet up with others. Then we will band together and build up a new and strong Jewish state.'

'That may be your wish, David, but you have a problem.'

'In what way, Mister Busek?'

'Amos, whom you met, and Ben will not be happy to be parted,' Kate answered for Hans. 'You see Amos, in Ben's eyes, has become his brother. Indeed if it was not for Amos befriending Ben in the concentration camp then he would not have survived.' David shook his head. 'Believe me, I do not know how the two of them survived all that happened. I also do not know, and I am amazed, that they managed to crawl their way out ... but

211

crawl they did... Amos hauling Ben every inch of the way. They shared everything ... even the misery ... the cruelty ... the inhumanity and the few crumbs that were thrown to them. You will be wondering Mister Sisken how I know all this?' Kate stopped to look at Hans before she could continue. 'I know all that worries Ben, even something that he could not confide to Amos. You see I have lost count of the times when in the stillness of the night I have held Ben in my arms when he was plagued by nightmares of all that has happened to him.' Kate sighed. 'At first the nightmares came every night, forcing him to relive the terrifying things he had seen, had endured. Thankfully, as he began to heal, their frequency lessened ... so much so that they are only occasional now. But make no mistake about it, Mister Sisken, whatever happened to Ben in the Bergen-Belsen concentration camp Amos saw him through it and always when he relives the horrors he has seen and endured he calls out for Amos.'

Before Kate could continue she heard the outside door open and just at that Aliza burst into the room and chanted, 'Mummy, I think it is time for you to hear my reading.' She then turned to address everyone in the room. 'I am a good reader now,' she said with a chuckle, 'and I can count and write my name.'

Kate nodded to Aliza but her eyes were fixed firmly on Ben, who had just entered the room. On seeing David a weeping Ben collapsed down on to the floor.

David's reaction was to rush over to Ben. 'It's okay. You are not dreaming.' David was now wiping the tears from Ben's eyes. 'But I am sorry to tell you, Benjamin, that we, you and I, are the only members of our family to survive.'

Kate now began to steer Aliza out of the room and just as she was about to pass over the threshold she turned. 'Hans, Amos,' she began as her eyes were drawn to Ben, 'I think that it is only right that Ben and David are left alone with each other.'

Two agonising hours passed before Ben opened the door and asked Kate, Amos and Hans to join him and his brother.

It was obvious that Ben had been crying and when David started to speak Ben hung his head. 'Mr and Mrs Busek, firstly I wish to say how grateful I am for the care you have taken of Benjamin.' Hans was about to interrupt David but he put up his hand to indicate that he had more to say and he then blundered on with, 'My thanks are especially for you Mrs Busek because you are not of our faith but from what Ben has told me you are obviously a good person ... possibly I think a practising Christian.'

Kate was incensed and no one could stop her from saying, 'David Sisken, I did not take on your brother because I am a Christian. And let's get it straight from the start, you are not the only one in this room who had to endure losing your whole family. My husband did. Oh yes, his wife and children were all killed and when he saw the plight of the children who had survived he wished to help them, heal them. So we agreed to foster one of the Jewish refugees. But when we decided to take Amos he came as a package with

Ben. Since their arrival in our home, religion has had nothing to do with how we treat them. Before I am a Christian I am foremost a human being who looked at three children ... three very damaged children and we, that is my husband and I, decided there and then that we had to help them. Mother them. Love them. Nurse them back to some sort of normality.'

David was obviously taken aback by Kate's direct manner and as soon as she stopped speaking he said, 'Please accept my apology. I did not mean to offend you. But I belong to a group who intend to go to Israel and help build up that country. Benjamin will be leaving your care and he will go with us and he also wishes that Amos would join us.'

Flopping back against the wall Kate cried, 'Oh no, I have grown to love these boys. Please leave them here with us at least until they finish their education. Your brother is very bright. He will go on to university.' Panic was now rising up in her chest and choking her. She just could not accept that she would lose Amos and Ben – especially Ben who was her special boy, her miracle boy, the boy who had trusted her with his secrets. Stuttering, she added, 'They have a privileged education at George Heriot's. Education is so important, especially to Ben.' She wished she could say to David Sisken that Ben, who because of the German programme where Jewish males were sterilised, might be like herself and never hold his own child in his arms. But she couldn't because Ben had told only her his shameful, as he saw it, secret about the dreadful surgical procedures

214

that were carried out on him.

Hans had now moved over to comfort Kate and very quietly he said, 'David, I know we should avenge what was inflicted on us. But I worry that in doing so we may destroy ourselves ... lose our humanity. Also I know Israel will have to be fought for ... here the boys live in peace. They are not fully recovered enough, in my opinion, to be taken from our loving care.'

David nodded. 'Mr Busek, I accept that you are entitled to your point of view, however I have already stated what has been agreed concerning Benjamin. I will call tomorrow to collect the boys. All that requires to be done now is that we arrange a time ... let's say about ten tomorrow morning.'

On their arrival back at the hospital to start their late shift Kitty and Dotty drew up abruptly when the duty porter called out, 'Nurse Anderson, a telegram and a letter have arrived for you.'

Frowning, Kitty turned to Dotty. 'Hope it's not bad news.'

Several seconds ticked by and Kitty just kept staring at the yellow envelope. 'Look Kitty, the only way you will find out what the gram says is to open it,' Dotty quipped. 'Here, if you haven't the courage give it over to me.'

Shaking her head Kitty tore open the envelope. As she read the contents her frown disappeared and was slowly replaced by a smug smile. 'Oh Dotty, it is from my darling boy. Look,' she cried passing the telegram over to Dotty.

Immediately Dotty began to read aloud from it.

'Congratulations. And top of the class at that. Did you get the important letter I sent you last week? It has instructions in it.' Dotty hesitated. 'Instructions! What kind of instructions?'

'It will just be about my travelling to Canada.'

'Oh, that will be what's in the letter.'

Kitty looked at the Canadian postmark and she grinned from ear to ear. 'But here,' she said glancing up at the clock, 'look at the time. The letter will have to keep until I come off duty tonight.'

Friday night shifts were always busy in Leith Hospital especially in Accident and Emergency where Kitty and Dotty were on duty.

By the end of the shift Kitty was completely drained of all energy. She had only one desire and that was to flop down on her bed and drift off to sleep. Slipping her hand underneath her apron she felt for her precious letter that every so often during her shift she had covertly stroked. Now in the privacy of her room her first desire was to open the letter and start reading it. Then she thought, *No, I must have a bath.* So she went along to the bathroom and filled the bath with warm water, which she then scented with a whole Radox bath cube. Whilst she lay in the comforting suds her mind relaxed and she became consumed by sunny thoughts of her impending wedding day. After half an hour she reluctantly got out of the bath and towel dried herself before liberally dusting her body with Yardley's talcum powder. She had done this because even although her Dougal would not actually be with her when she read his letter he would be in her mind. Donning her flannelette pyjamas she chuckled. They were so

216

different from the black silk negligee that she had splashed out on – the gorgeous creation that she would wear on her wedding night.

Once she had snuggled up in bed with her head supported by two pillows she opened the letter.

By the time she reached over to switch off her bedside table lamp she had read, and read, and reread the letter over and over again. It was just so important to her to digest every word so that she was sure that she understood exactly what he wished her to do.

Kitty awoke early in the morning. She didn't feel quite rested but she knew that further sleep would evade her. This being so, and because she was not on duty until early afternoon, she decided to go and visit her Aunt Kate. Dear, dependable Aunt Kate who throughout all of her life had always been there to listen to her – to advise her – to pick her up when she had been kicked down. This all being true she was anxious to get to Kate as soon as possible so after hurriedly dressing, she quickly left the hospital.

She had just emerged into Great Junction Street when she became aware that the bus was arriving at the stop so she quickly jumped aboard. After alighting from the bus in Lochend Road she checked her watch and noted that it was now nearly ten thirty so she began to sprint towards her aunt's house. Whilst she was running she tried to shift her thoughts from Dougal's written suggestions. As she neared her aunt's house, that was situated in East Restalrig Terrace, she was thinking how wise her Aunt Kate and Uncle Hans had been to follow her dad and Connie's example and pur-chase a bigger house. A house that was about the same size as her father and Connie's and afforded them more living space. Both houses, although larger, were in no way ostentatious. Oh no, the houses were homes – homes that were always clean and fresh but in no way sanitised – homes in which you never felt you should take your shoes off at the door. It was also gratifying for Kitty to acknowledge that Amos, Ben and Aliza had been fortunate enough to have been fostered by Aunt Kate and Uncle Hans. Yes, she agreed as she opened the gate to her aunt's path, these poor abused children now lived in a comfortable home where they were valued and loved.

Aware that Hans would have left to attend to his shop around eight thirty and that being so her aunt would be alone with the children, Kate opened the unlocked front door and as she bounded into the house she cried, 'Just me, Aunty Kate.' However, when she advanced into the bright, airy kitchen she became concerned be-cause her aunt looked so tired and washed out.

'You feeling all right?'

'It's nothing, Kitty,' a melancholy Kate replied. 'I didn't sleep well last night. But what brings you here today? I wasn't expecting you until Monday.'

Kitty pulled out a dining chair and she sat her-self down opposite Kate. Without saying a word, Kitty fished Dougal's letter from her handbag and she slipped it over the table towards Kate.

Immediately, Kate took the letter from its enve-lope and, like Kitty, when she first read it she appeared to become dumbfounded. Also, like Kitty, she read it another three times before she spat, 'Is he all there?'

Kitty shrugged.

Looking at the letter again, Kate decided to read it aloud so that her besotted niece could hear just what a ridiculous prat Dougal was. Slowly articulating every syllable she began.

*My Darling Kitty*

*I am counting not only the days but every minute until we are together again. I am just so in love with you and I wish you to know that I will never, ever love anyone the way I love you.*

*As to our wedding day, I am afraid I have to tell you that there will have to be a short delay. You see I got rather mixed up with a young lady called Mona. Her father, a bully of a man who is a Chief Super-intendent in the Canadian Mounted Police here in Ontario, insisted that I marry his Mona as she had made herself pregnant by me.*

*What I am trying to convey to you is that I will require to remain married to Mona until after the child is born. Then I will ask her for a divorce. You see her father is insistent that his grandchild is not born illegitimate. I am sure that you will be able to under-stand that. And, indeed, I would not wish a child that I had possibly fathered to go through life with that stigma.*

*Back to us, nothing has changed, except that you don't need to be rushing out to Canada. But for my happiness' sake you must come. I assure you that as soon as possible I will divorce Mona and then you and I can wed. In the circumstances I think that perhaps we should settle in New Brunswick, where no one will be aware that I have been married before.*

*Please, please, my darling, write to me and advise me when you intend to arrive in Ontario.*

*Love you always. Believe me you are the only woman I have every truly loved.*

*Your devoted and loving,*

*Dougal*

Kate began to scratch her head. Kitty looked so lost and heartbroken that Kate was sure that if Dougal had been standing in the room right now she would have done him physical injury.

Speaking in a hushed voice, Kitty asked, 'Aunty Kate, what should I do?'

'Do?' Kate screeched. 'Don't be stupid ... you are not stupid. So there is no requirement for you to ask me what you should do.'

An uneasy silence fell between aunt and niece. Both were battling to keep their emotions in check.

Kate eventually stated, 'Right, you have had enough time to think. Now tell me exactly what you propose to do about this.' She then lifted the letter, and with unconcealed contempt, she threw it over the table towards Kitty.

'Write to him and say that I am not coming to Canada now or at any time in the future. I will enclose the engagement ring that he gave me in the envelope.' She now removed the ring from her finger and placed it in the envelope that had brought his letter. 'In the correspondence I will tell him never, ever to contact me again.'

'Good. Now, as to what you must do right now.

Well, I'm afraid that it will mean you eating a large dollop of humble pie.' Kitty nodded. She had already worked that one out for herself.

'So before you go on duty today make a point of having a meeting with Matron and ask her if you may withdraw your resignation.'

'I know I should, but I just can't,' Kitty whispered. 'Everyone will be laughing at me behind my back. Oh Aunty Kate, I made so much fuss about not serving my first year as a staff nurse in Leith Hospital. Can't you see ... it will all be so humiliating?'

'It will be a seven-day wonder. Everyone has problems.'

Kitty nodded. 'I know that. And this change of plans has highlighted my other problem in that I don't have a home.'

'That's not true ... you could always come and stay with Hans and myself.'

'Aunty Kate, you are not a lady almoner. You have enough on your hands with Amos, Ben and Aliza. And you are not responsible for housing me.'

Kate leaned back in her chair. Tears gathered at the back of her eyes – tears she was determined not to allow to flow. 'I do have room for you. You see, just before you arrived, Ben's elder brother David took Ben and Amos away. I think it is his intention to settle them in Israel.'

'What?' Kitty exclaimed. 'Oh Aunty, you have enough to be coping with today. I should not have come here and burdened you further with my problems.'

Sniffing, and taking out a handkerchief that was

tucked in under her sleeve, Kate shook her head. 'My dear Kitty, you are never a bother to me. You couldn't be. Before I met Hans my life would have been so lonely and meaningless if you had not been in it.'

Lifting her hand to cover her mouth Kate thought, *Why on earth do some people think that they have the right to run roughshod over other people? Why do they never stop to think about the effects that their selfish cruel actions will have on others?*

The pressure that Kitty used to knock on Matron's door was far from robust. Nonetheless, Matron heard it and immediately called out, 'Come in.'

When she saw that the caller was Kitty, her face froze. Then in a voice that sank the temperature in the room by ten degrees, she snorted, 'And what rules,' she said, rolling the 'R', 'do you wish to be set aside today?'

'Matron,' Kitty gulped, 'it is very difficult for me to ask but I wondered if you could please assist me and allow me to withdraw...?'

'From all your obligations right now,' exploded Matron.

'No, I would like to withdraw my resignation.'

Matron looked perplexed. 'And why? I mean, only last week you were of the opinion that Canada couldn't survive without your expertise.'

Kitty flinched. Having Matron grant her wish was going to be more difficult than she thought. This being the case, she decided to tell the truth, the whole truth and nothing but the truth. Fishing in her uniform pocket she withdrew Dougal's letter, which she then pushed over the desk towards Matron.

Matron lifted the letter and began reading from it. Kitty was then quite shocked when she announced, 'This is the most cynical letter I have ever read.'

Without being granted Matron's permission Kitty flopped down on the guest chair next to Matron's desk. 'What do you mean, Matron?' she whimpered.

'Just that this letter is a cruel "Dear John".' Matron snorted and huffed before adding, 'And is nothing more and nothing less than that.'

'No. He states that I should come over and wait until...'

'And what decent person in their right mind would do as he asks? No. No. Nurse Anderson, this letter has been written in such a way that he wishes to be released from his promise to you. For goodness sake he is now a married man and his wife is pregnant. And as to him being forced to marry the lady, if you are not convinced by what I am saying, find out the exact date of the wedding.'

Kitty felt embarrassed – she knew she looked, because she herself felt – a first-class fool.

Matron, obviously sorry for the predicament that Kitty found herself in, sighed before quietly saying, 'Now Anderson, I am speaking to you confidentially. You see some who have reached senior ranks within our hospital have been, let's say, let down rather than jilted, and they have gone on to make a very successful career for themselves and their lives have been more than fulfilled.'

It was the manner in which Matron had uttered the words that led Kitty to correctly guess that she was talking about herself. An admission that somewhere in her very distant past Matron too had been deserted by a lover.

Several minutes ticked by with no words passing between the two women. Kitty could see that the Matron was deep in thought.

When Matron did decide to break the silence Kitty was so surprised that all she could do was stay silent. 'Now, Nurse Anderson,' Matron began, although she appeared to be talking to the back wall, 'it would be very difficult for you to continue to work here as a staff nurse. You have to command respect and Dougal McNeill, for reasons best known to him, has made that impossible for you.' Kitty almost screamed in protest but she breathed in deeply and prepared herself for the rest of what Matron would say. 'I will contact my opposite number in the Eastern General Hospital at Seafield, a very competent lady, but then she was trained here, and it won't take much persuasion on my part for her to allow you to do your one-year staff nurse training there. On completion of that you can then apply to do six months' midwifery. After that you will have to decide for yourself what you wish to do with your life. But please do not allow a scoundrel like Dougal McNeill to undermine your confidence.'

Kitty nodded.

'You have three weeks to work here but how about you go on holiday next week. And when you return you will go straight to the Eastern General Hospital.'

'Are you sure that you can arrange all that?'

'Yes. Matron there and I have a good working relationship. You are a very good nurse and she is short right now of excellent nurses, especially in the wards that are dealing with the servicemen who have returned with tropical diseases.'

Kitty was silently crying. This woman who had always seemed to her to be a ferocious dragon had seen how humiliating it would have been for her to admit to the staff of Leith Hospital that Dougal had jilted her – made her a laughing stock and she had gone out of her way to make things as easy as she possibly could for her.

'Where will you go on holiday?' was Matron's last question for Kitty.

'I think down to visit my friend Laura who now lives in Cornwall. She also has her little nephew with her there.'

Matron nodded. The audience was over.

Dotty was just about to go on duty when Kitty arrived at the nurses' home. Immediately Kitty confidentially advised Dotty of all the day's goings-on.

'The unfeeling, arrogant swine,' were Dotty's first remarks, before saying, 'You're going to Cornwall to see Laura?' Kitty nodded. 'Then, as I too am on annual leave from tomorrow, I'm coming with you.'

'Good. And as Laura now has her own guest house there will be plenty of room for both of us.'

It was a very long week for Kate and Hans. They deliberately never spoke of the boys. Aliza, who required quite a bit of reassuring, kept them busy and to help, Connie allowed Rosebud to stay over most nights. The nights that Rosebud did not stay Kate knew that around midnight Aliza would be standing at the side of her and Hans' bed saying, 'Mummy, I am frightened without Amos and Ben being here, can I come in and sleep with you and Papa Hans?'

Exactly one week after the boys had gone Kate was sitting staring into space whilst listening to Hans playing the piano. He had so loved playing with Amos, but that joy in his life was now gone forever.

In the recent past, it was their custom not to lock the doors because the boys continually came and went. To Kate, who so felt the loss of their boys, locking the door before they retired for the night would somehow, in her tortured mind, be locking the boys out of her life. Indeed, turning the key early would have been a signal to her that the boys were lost to her forever.

The brilliant sunset of the Saturday evening was flooding into the room and it seemed somehow to meet up with Hans' haunting music. Mesmerised, Kate turned when she felt a cold blast of air as the door opened. She then pinched herself just to make sure that she was not dreaming because there stood Amos and Ben.

'Mama Kate,' was all Ben said whilst Amos went over and placed his hands firmly on Hans' shoulders before joining him on the extended piano stool.

'What happened?' Kate cried, as she got up and took Ben into a tight embrace.

'Like you, Mama Kate, I just couldn't do it.'

'You mean you couldn't leave Aliza?'

Ben and Amos both nodded before Ben said, 'Not only Aliza, we just couldn't leave you and Papa Hans. We are family now. You made us what we are today. Not wholly healed yet but confident enough to be well on our way.'

Amos put his hand over Hans'. 'Papa,' he began, 'I like the peace and quiet that is always around you. I like how you never make me feel that I am a burden to you ... that I am a poor substitute for your sons.'

Tears flowing, Hans turned around to face Ben full on before mumbling, 'But Ben, your brother was adamant that you must go with him.'

'That is so, Papa. So we promised him that when we finish our schooling we will think long and hard about what we wish to do.'

Kate and Hans both smiled. Both knew that by the time their articulate boys finished their schooling they would be making their own decisions. Just like they had done today in coming home – home to where they were loved and cherished.

# PART SEVEN

## MAY 1949

Kitty was busy packing up her belongings when Dotty literally bounced into the room and exclaimed, 'I have just gone through a six-hour labour and thank goodness that it is my last one.' She then held up her right hand to show Kitty some scars where someone had dug their nails into her. 'Got these souvenirs before I had time to get my gloves on and dish out the gas and air. Packing already?'

'Yeah, I want to dump most of this at my dad's house, have a quick visit to Eric in Saughton Prison, then I am on my way to have eight days, eight days do you hear, just lazing about in Carlyon Bay.'

'Oh, so you've decided to give Laura a visit.' Kitty nodded. 'Suppose that means you are putting off looking for a job until you get back?'

Kitty pulled a face before saying, 'And here talking about finding a job ... you'll need to find one too so which hospitals are you going to apply to?' She stopped to inhale deeply before exclaiming with delight, 'Now that, like me, you are not only a state registered nurse, but also a midwife?'

Biting her lip, Dotty cast her eyes downward. 'Kitty, with our exams and whatnot over, and as

229

we were on our last few days here... I didn't tell you but my mum is terminally ill. I am therefore duty-bound to go back to Ireland to nurse her.' She hesitated before brightly adding, 'But with the qualifications I have now, I'll have no trouble finding a job there. The problem is, if there is a need for me to stay, I might never ever get back here where I have learned so much, been so happy. Met this idiot of a girl who I could confide anything to, only problem with her is that when I first met her she didn't like older men courting her and now she has become a ... man hater.'

'Rubbish. I love my dad, my brothers, my nephews, even Eric.'

Dotty got up and began brushing her hair. As she looked in the mirror, she also saw Kitty's reflection. *Five years,* she thought, *have passed since I first met you at the door of the nurses' home in Leith Hospital.* She smiled as she remembered that they had just been naive nineteen going on twenty-year-olds, thrilled to be taking up a career in nursing. Today they, at twenty-four, going on twenty-five, were fully qualified nurses and the time had come for them to go their separate ways.

'Please, Kitty,' Dotty pleaded, as she stopped grooming her hair, 'don't let a weasel like Dougal McNeil have you die an old maid. He's dross but believe me there's plenty of gold out there.'

The honking of a taxi cab put an end to the girls' banter. Neither wished to leave the other so as they quickly and tightly embraced Kitty said, 'You know where my dad's house is and you know Connie, so if ever you need to get in touch with me urgently, go there, and my family will help you and they will know where I am, and I will come running.'

'Nurse, Nurse,' Dotty said in a voice imitating Sister Tutor, 'there are only two reasons that should cause you to run, one is fire and the other is haemorrhage!'

Reaching her destination and paying off the taxi driver, Kitty was surprised that Connie did not come to the door to meet her. Thankfully, the taxi driver, who liked pretty young women, helped her inside with her several suitcases, books, pictures, cushions, etc.

After dumping all her earthly belongings down on the hall floor, Kitty advanced into the kitchen. On seeing Connie, she gasped and then had to swallow her fist to keep herself from laughing out loud. 'In the name of all that is holy, what have you done to your bonnie hair?'

'Don't laugh, Kitty, you see I gave myself a Toni home perm last night and I don't think I got it quite right.'

Still stifling her giggles, Kitty chuckled. 'Didn't get it quite right? You can say that again. Oh Connie, you look as if you have had your fingers in an electric socket. What my dad will say when he comes home on Friday, I just don't know.'

Connie slumped down on a chair. 'Wish he was coming on Friday. Only comes home every second week now... Oh Kitty, ever since he got that long-legged secretary-type lassie ... well I miss him and I need him now.' Listening to Connie's heart-breaking story quickly wiped the smile off Kitty's face. 'Trying to make myself look good for him was all I was trying to do. Made a mess of that too, haven't I?'

It didn't take Kitty long to decide that she would have to do something about what had gone wrong in her father's household. 'Connie,' she began gently but firmly, 'feeling sorrow for yourself and not getting to...' Kitty looked about the kitchen, which was clean enough but a jumbled mess, 'grips with the housework isn't going to help. And you have two children to look after and okay Rosebud is nine going on ninety now so she just needs fed and a little supervision, but Jackie, your very own child, is just four and the wee soul won't be at school until August.'

'Nursery.'

'Doesn't matter if it is school or nursery, she is still young, and with Daddy out of her life five days a week...' Connie was about to protest and point out that he was only home two days in fourteen of late but Kitty put up her hand. 'So I am asking you to give yourself a shake because, believe me, I know my father and I also know that he will be home this Friday. These weekends he has not been here in Edinburgh that will be...' Kitty stopped to think what she should say next. 'That will be because of some urgent House of Commons business or something else ... like that but it will be all over now.' Kitty then started to put on a show of being light-hearted and as she nudged Connie, she simpered, 'So to make sure that you all have a good weekend together start getting the house ready for the master's return.' Connie nodded. 'Sorry I can't roll up my sleeves and help you. This afternoon I just have to visit Eric.'

The mention of Eric's name brought a spark of life back to Connie. 'Is it true that he will be getting released soon?'

'Yes. If he continues to be the model prisoner he is he will be free in about three months' time. But when he is released he won't be staying here. Intends, he does, to make a home for himself and Billy in Cornwall. I think that is for the best because he will be near Laura and she will look out for them. Also nobody will know his past or taunt Billy about his mum and dad.' Clucking her tongue as she tried to make sure she had covered everything for Connie, Kitty finally said, 'And did I say to you that I will be leaving early in the morning because I must catch the early train?' She paused. She didn't like deliberately lying to Connie but Connie would feel humiliated if she knew that Kitty, before going to Cornwall, would firstly be travelling to London to see her father. The visit she would make to him tomorrow would only ever be known to the two of them. After London, it would be full steam ahead for Carlyon Bay in Cornwall.

It had been her intention just to have a short visit with Eric, but Eric was quite excited about the prospect of his impending release so a quick half hour became a long hour.

Over and over again Eric had asked Kitty if she thought that his release would go ahead sooner rather than later. Then he went on to outline all the plans that he had made for a new life for himself and Billy. Kitty had to, at one point, gently say to Eric that Billy didn't really know him now and therefore, at first, he would have to allow time for a relationship to develop between them. Eric, however, countered her concerns by reminding Kitty that Laura had always made sure that Billy knew that he had a daddy and that soon they would be together. As London was uppermost in her mind she eventually just shrugged and finally managed to diplomatically end her visit with Eric. Her parting words to him were, 'Your Billy is a clever little boy and you'll soon find out that he is more than able to give you a run for your money on the mouth organ.'

She was still thinking about Eric and Billy when she arrived at the prison's outside door. But Eric and Billy's future problems vanished from her thoughts when she looked out at the horrendous, spectacular thunderstorm that had besieged the city.

Looking down at her sandal-shod feet, she sighed. There was no way she could go out into the deluge, especially as she was only wearing a thin summer jacket.

'Quite a surprise,' a male voice said.

Turning to answer, Kitty was surprised to find Felix Martin, the advocate who had prosecuted in Eric's case. 'Oh hello, it's you.'

'Yes it is. And I was just making sure that it was you. I mean you are Miss Anderson or Mrs...?'

'Still Miss Anderson, I am happy to say.'

Although surprised and very pleased at her answer, Felix only asked, 'You have no transport of your own?'

Kitty just giggled and shook her head.

'In that case could I offer you a lift home, Miss Anderson?'

'That would be just great. But I could only allow you to do that if you would call me Kitty.' He laughed. 'You can laugh but someone saying Miss Anderson makes me feel rather old and dowdy.'

He didn't answer her but he did think that he could never, ever imagine a time when he would think that she was old and dowdy. Without another word he opened up his large umbrella and together they dashed over to his parked car.

'Now where is it that you reside?'

'Normally in the nurses' home but for the next few weeks ... that is until I find another job, I am lodging at my father's house on the Ferry Road, just opposite the Goldenacre playing fields.'

He laughed before replying, 'Your father and I are practically neighbours. My home is the last house before the church in Inverleith Gardens.'

'That's just great because I really do have to get home quickly. You see I'm catching the London train in the morning.'

'You are going to London?'

'Just a small detour for a day or two but then...' She hunched her shoulders with delight. 'I will be Carlyon Bay in Cornwall bound where I will have about five wonderful days holidaying ... just doing nothing.' She babbled on, 'To me, sheer heaven is getting my deckchair close up to the large rocky cliffs on the beach and getting a book out.'

'You like reading then?'

'I do.'

They were now coming down into Goldenacre. Quite innocently Kitty said, 'Hope my step-mother has some nice food ready for me. I haven't had time to eat since breakfast.'

She was then surprised when Felix did a three-point turn with his car and then started to head back up past the Botanic Gardens.

'Where are we going?'

He smiled, and she couldn't be sure, but she thought he winked at her. 'I haven't eaten all day either,' he chortled, 'so as I know a charming little restaurant, ah here we are... Now please, Kitty, let me treat you to your supper.'

Kitty smiled as she boarded the London train because there in the second carriage was a vacant south-facing corner seat that she could tuck herself into and either watch the countryside pass by, read her book or catch up on some sleep.

The noise of the train, as it clickety-clack, clickety-clack, clickety-clacked its way southward had a soporific effect on Kitty. Drifting in and out of sleep she went over the happenings of the day before.

Firstly, it was so sad to have said goodbye to Dotty. Then she had discovered Connie upset about her dad's treatment of her, and indeed she was so concerned that she was now London bound. She then thought on her visit to Eric, before finally allowing her meeting with Felix Martin to dominate her thoughts. Thinking of this man awakened such pleasurable feelings within her that she had to make herself think about mundane things before these feelings became, what was alien to her, sensual. She did try to pass away time by thinking about which hospitals she would apply to for a position but her mind kept drifting back again and again to Felix. She even tried to say to herself that this man was at least ten years older than she was so what could they have in common? Okay, she admitted, he had taken pity on her, and had treated her to a very nice meal but by the time he had dropped her off at her father's house, what did she know about him? Nothing! She grimaced as she admitted, well there was one thing that she knew about him now and that was that he was very good at his job. How did she know that? Well, she had spent two and a half hours in his company and he had managed to have her tell him all about herself and her life but he had expertly made sure that she got to know nothing about him. Finally, she thought about how it was four years since they had first briefly met yet somehow he remembered her. She smiled, thinking wouldn't it be nice if somehow he had always been hovering in the background.

Kings Cross Station was an eye-opener for Kitty. She was so amazed by the constant hustle and bustle that she began to have second thoughts about her visit. After all, other than going to see Laura in Cornwall, she had never really been out of Leith.

Lugging her case towards the left luggage she deposited it there before advancing out into the front street just carrying her overnight bag. Looking about she wondered where all the traffic of buses, cars, lorries and taxis had come from.

The problem perplexing her was that she had no idea which bus she should take to get to her Father's bedsit. She stood and assessed the situation. London, she thought, was such a noisy, busy, frightening city that she concluded it was no time to be thrifty so she hailed a taxi.

Opening the taxi door the driver asked, 'Where to, love?'

'Seventy-two Oban Street. I think it might be somewhere near the House of Commons.'

The taxi driver pushed the "for hire" flag down before saying, 'Nope. Oban Street is nowhere near the Houses of Parliament.' He scratched his head before adding, 'But mind you, as the crow flies, it's not that far.'

When the taxi driver drew up at Oban Street, Kitty paid the exact fare the driver asked for. She added no tip because she thought he knew that she was a stranger in town so had taken her via anywhere he could, just to bump up his earnings.

Once she had alighted from the cab she glanced about. To be truthful, Oban Street appeared to be no Buckingham Palace, but then it was no Skid Row either.

Advancing to the door of number seventy-two she could see that on the ground floor, where Connie had said her father had his flat, there were five doors leading off. Checking the nameplates she was pleased to discover that number three had her father's name on it.

Breathing in deeply she knocked sharply on the door.

After a minute she heard a young female voice calling, 'Cooee, cooee, Johnny boy. You're early.

Suppose you couldn't wait to get home to me.'

The door was then opened by a black-haired, scantily clad, young woman. Her broad grin was replaced by a deep frown when she saw Kitty. Tutting and sighing, she came further out of the doorway and pointed to the next door on the right. 'That there is Charlie Spring's place. Wish to goodness he would give you "ladies" the right address.'

The lady then went to close the door but was prevented from doing so by Kitty pushing into the room. 'Here, what do you think you're doing? This is private property. Johnny Anderson will not half be furious if he finds you here.'

'You're right there. But the one person he will not find here when he gets back is you. What's your name...?'

'Molly, but Johnny Boy calls me Candy.'

Kitty couldn't hide her disgust. 'That right,' she hissed. 'Well, Molly, Candy, or whatever your name is, just pack your bags and go.'

'But I am Mister Anderson's bona fide researcher...'

Looking disdainfully at the turned down bed-settee, Kitty gritted her teeth. 'That right?' she sweetly emphasised. 'Well, take it from me I am his bona fide daughter and as he will no longer be requiring any further research of a horizontal nature I am terminating your employment.'

'You can't do that.'

'Well if you would rather that I get rid of you some other way?'

'You mean murder me!' Candy gulped whilst backing away from Kitty.

'It would be a very last resort... But yes,' Kitty, who was now in a mood to tease this young woman, uttered as she ran her right index finger over her neck. 'But then the choice is yours.'

'You wouldn't dare cut my throat,' Candy gulped as she began to distance herself, even further, from Kitty.

Kitty just nodded as she slinked closer and closer to Candy.

'But I know you wouldn't because you're so wrong about Johnny Anderson... He doesn't have any children.'

'That right?' Kitty hollered as she swallowed hard to quell her utter exasperation. 'Now let me tell you that when he was married to my mother he fathered Bobby, Jack, Dave, Rosebud and you know about me, and if that's not enough to be going on with, his second wife, Connie, has a little angel of a daughter by him.'

'You're having me on.'

'I can assure you I am not. And furthermore, from next Monday my father's administrative needs will be supplied by a male clerk and researcher.'

Before either Kitty or Candy could continue there was a light rap on the door and a male voice simpered, 'Cooee, cooee, it's me, Candy, baby.'

Johnny then leapt into the room, giving a demonstration of a rutting stag and shouting, 'I am ready to fight for you ... even die for you.' But the smile died on his face when he lifted his eyes and he was confronted with Kitty.

He then stuttered, 'Oh, em, oo, oh, ah, hah.'

'Yes,' Kitty calmly said, although she was

frenzied with rage. 'Oh, em, ah, oo to you too. Now I have already politely asked that Miss Candy not only vacate this bedsit right now but also your life. What I expect from you, *Daddy*, is just a nod to confirm that is exactly what she should do ... otherwise her blood will be spilt on the carpet. And I am sure you wouldn't want that.'

Johnny was now gasping like a fish out of water. But when he saw the look on Kitty's face, which reminded him of his late mother, he meekly bobbed his head. In fact, he was so keen to appease her that he resembled a fairground nodding dog.

It then took Candy just five minutes to gather up her belongings and when the door banged shut behind her Kitty's full attention landed on her father.

'What on earth do you think you are playing at? Have you forgotten that you are a socialist and not a Tory?'

'Don't know what you mean.'

'Just that it is Conservatives who create sexual scandals with women young enough to be their granddaughters, and that socialists, when they wish to commit political suicide, usually put their hands in the till.'

Johnny was about to reply when Kitty, who had to restrain herself from hitting him, added, 'And have you thought of what this will do to Connie? Yesterday the poor soul was so down about you ... and don't think that when you arrived home stinking of stale cologne and too tired to even talk to her that she didn't think ... or know ... what you had been up to. Dad, you are a first class numbskull... Honestly, how could you be so stupid as to put all you have worked for at stake for a ... a ... at best, a good-time girl? That Candy, Dad, is younger than me.' Kitty's eyes rolled before she spluttered, 'And have you any idea what the gutter-press headlines will look like when she sells them her story?'

Again Johnny tried to put up a defence but Kitty hissed, 'Oh Dad, you have so completely lost it that you don't realise that the next General Election is, at the most, only nine months away? Who in middle-class Wardie, Davidson's Mains, Silverknowes and all around Granton will vote for you if you leave Connie or she throws you out ... and for an affair with a bimbo like Candy? And have you thought about where you will find a job that pays you one thousand pounds a year? And don't forget that that salary pays the mortgage on Ferry Road and keeps Rosebud and Jackie in shoes?'

Kitty was spent and tears sprang to her eyes. She just couldn't believe that her dad, born and bred in Leith by her grandmother, could be behaving like a first-class ass.

Now that Johnny could get a word in, he adopted a rather superior tone to say, 'Miss, I think you should remember who you are speaking to and as your father I deserve respect.'

'That right? Well as far as I am concerned respect is something that you earn.' She then lifted up a pair of silk stockings that Candy had left behind and she forcibly threw them in her father's face.

The following morning the atmosphere between father and daughter was still cooler than Antarctica.

On arrival at the Edinburgh train platform, Johnny, who couldn't wait to see the back of Kitty, uttered in a superior tone of voice, 'I best get aboard.'

'Fine. But first there are a few things I still have to go over with you.'

'With all you had to say last night that's not possible.'

Kitty ignored her father's sarcasm and proceeded to say, 'I am aware that you think you can get away with anything ... and that is not all your fault. No. No. The women in your life who have always allowed you to get off scot-free are also to blame.'

'What do you mean?'

'Like when Mum died, you dumped all your responsibilities on me, a fifteen-year-old slip of a lassie. And, if it hadn't been for Granny, Aunt Kate and dear Connie, I would not have been able to cope with a newborn baby and a household during rationing time. Now poor gullible Connie holds the fort while you play the big-shot politician.' Johnny huffed. 'Oh yes, Dad, she does and she was the one who sorted our Davy out.'

'I hope you don't think that getting him to start courting a lassie from the Baptists is...'

'His saviour? Yes I do. Believe me, Joy is most certainly that, Dad. But back to you, from now on you won't dump your responsibilities on any of us.' Winking and cocking her head towards him she continued with, 'Time to grow up and be the "big guy" with your family because in the end that's all that you will be left with.' Kitty inhaled deeply before going on. 'Now I won't mention to anyone about what you got up to down here. Not for your sake, but I not only love Connie I also owe her. Therefore, I cannot stand by and see her humiliated. Finally, when you get off the train, go and buy some flowers and chocolates and a couple of things for Rosebud and Jackie. And tomorrow night get Davy and that lovely wee lassie, Joy, he's nuts about, to babysit and then take Connie out for a meal.'

'Go to Costa's chippie?'

'Definitely not Costa's chippie. Up from the Botanic Gardens, on the right hand side, you'll find a small, family run restaurant. Romantic place. And you make sure that Connie knows, not so much that she has you back, but that you never two-timed her.'

'Know something,' Johnny spat in reply. 'I'm always promoting the education of women and saying it is the way forward ... well miss, the educating of you has certainly been a stick to break my back.'

Kitty chuckled. Johnny then jumped aboard with Kitty's final words ringing in his ears. 'And don't ever think of straying again because I really quite like getting up to date with my reading on long train journeys.'

It was early evening when Kitty's train pulled into St Austell. Jumping from the train and then lugging off her case, Kitty looked about the platform. No welcoming committee.

She was just considering asking the directions to the bus station when Mike Bailey sprinted into view.

'Whoa. Whoa. There's no fire,' Kitty said before squinting behind him. 'Laura busy with the bed and breakfast?'

'Yes and no. She had a doctor's appointment but I dropped her off home to get our meal started.' Kitty looked puzzled. 'Anything wrong?'

'No. She just had some check-ups to get done and our neighbour said she would look after Billy when he got in from school.'

During the run to Carlyon Bay, in what Mike called his reliable old banger, the conversation was light and when Sea Road loomed into view a broad smile came to Kitty's face.

The car had just drawn to a halt when Laura came out to greet Kitty. Kitty's eyes popped.

'Here, Laura, what's this with the smock? Are you...?'

Laura grabbed Kitty by both hands and they did a little jig about the pathway.

'You never said.'

'No. I am just three months.'

'Then why are you wearing a smock now?'

'Just want the whole world to know that Mike and I are going to be someone's mum and dad.'

They were now indoors and Laura was leading Kitty to her room when Kitty whispered in her ear, 'And does the dragon in Trinity, your mother-in-law, know?'

Laughing, Laura shook her head. 'As you know, she washed her hands of Mike when he married me. Her attitude to me and my family was the

245

reason that he applied for and got the surveyor's job down here. So I don't care if she never sees her grandchildren. But then, would she wish to be a granny, a proper granny, to a child,' Laura lovingly rubbed her hand over her stomach, 'who had been brought into this world by the sister of a monster?'

Kitty turned and took Laura into her arms. 'I've missed you so.'

Laura brightened. 'Now do tell why you changed the day of your arrival?'

'Don't ask. All I will tell you is that my idiot father has been thinking he's Casanova.'

'So you had to go to London and sort him out?'

Kitty shrugged. 'Yes. But I wouldn't take a bet on him saying no if another bird brain with legs that go on forever gives him the glad eye.'

Laughing, Laura replied, 'Come on Kitty, your dad will soon be pushing fifty and that's over the hill for true romance.'

Kitty pondered before asking, 'And a woman at twenty-five, Laura?'

'She's in her prime, Kitty ... a beautiful full-grown cherry ready for picking.'

Kitty spent the whole weekend with Laura, Mike and Billy. Billy had chatted to her about how it would soon be time for his dad to get out of hospital and then he would be able to come to Cornwall and they would go fishing together. When he said that, Kitty had bitten on her lip because Billy had reminded her of how Laura's dad and brother had always gone fishing. Lads' bonding time it had always been and she did so hope that it wasn't too late for Eric and Billy to form such a relationship.

On Monday morning the sun was high in the sky and Billy had just left for school when Laura announced that, as she was going to the antenatal exercise clinic, she thought Kitty should spend the day on Crinnis Beach. That was the beach just at the bottom of Sea Road. She and Mike would drop her off with a deckchair and she would stay there just relaxing and reading her book.

Kitty, with assistance from Mike, managed to anchor the chair so that the cliff face was at her back and she was looking out to the clear blue bay. No wonder, she thought, as she settled down for the morning, that they call this place the Cornish Riviera.

She did read for half an hour but then she decided to lift her face to be kissed by the sun. She sighed deeply as the warm rays relaxed her and she began reflecting on her life. As she became completely soporific she thought that, on the whole, it had not been such a bad one. Then she became aware that the sun was no longer toasting her. Opening her eyes, she expected to see the sun blocked out by a cloud, but she was faced with the figure of a tall man.

'Excuse me,' she said politely but feeling a bit put out, 'you are blocking my sunlight.'

He laughed uproariously. 'Oh, Miss Anderson, the last thing I would ever want to do is get in the way of your sunshine.'

Rising from a deckchair is always an ungainly activity and Kitty found herself clutching at the trousers of the man as she tried to steady herself and get up into an upright position.

As soon as she was steady, she half turned to see who the man, who obviously knew her well enough to know her name, was. On finding herself face to face with Felix Martin, she flopped back down on to the deckchair.

'What on earth are you doing here?' she cried as she got up off the seat again.

'Same as you ... enjoying a well-earned holiday.'

'No. When we had supper together you told me nothing about yourself, except that when I mentioned I was coming here to Carlyon Bay, you said that you always liked holidaying up in the Highlands or over in the Hebrides.' Kitty now squinted to look over the sand and towards the bright blue twinkling sea. 'And that sea dancing out there is the English Channel; it is definitely not the Minch.'

'I concur. But as to why I am here. You see, you spoke so enthusiastically about Carlyon Bay, I felt I just had to come and see it for myself.'

Kitty looked quizzically at Felix. She was sure he was not telling her the whole truth. What was more disconcerting was that she just couldn't suppress the feeling of intoxication that was washing over her because he was standing so near to her.

'And you are, of course, quite right. It is very beautiful.'

'And that is the sole reason why you took the train down here?'

'No. I came by car.'

'Car?'

'Yes. I had intended driving to Mallaig, boarding the ferry there and then touring the Isles of

Uist, but the desire to finish our little chat put that trip on the back-burner.'

'Oh,' teased Kitty, 'you mean you wish to tell me all about yourself?'

He shook his head. Telling anyone about himself was something he found very difficult. A silence had fallen between them and he could see that she was waiting for an answer.

Quietly, but firmly, he said, 'My mother always advised me that I should never confide to anyone any details about myself.'

Kitty shook her head. Why the secrecy, she wondered. Then she concluded that perhaps it was because he had been born out of wedlock. She then went on to think that his mother must have had means because how else could she have afforded his private-school fees and university tuition?

Whilst Kitty was trying to solve the mystery of what Felix had to hide he was thinking back to when he first began to realise that his being in this world was an embarrassment to most of his relatives, especially his mother's parents.

## FELIX'S STORY

As he grew up he never forgot the only words that he ever heard his grandfather utter. 'Anne,' he had said in a disdainful tone, 'I am very sorry but you have misunderstood our invitation. It was for you alone. We have no desire to accommodate a child that is ... let's put it nicely ... difficult for us to acknowledge. I am aware you thought that as we have allowed five years to pass since we asked you

249

to leave our home that we had perhaps ... well we haven't. It is also regrettable that he looks like me. Now if you wish to come back alone we would be happy to see you.'

Felix's mother had then grabbed him by the hand as she prepared to leave her parents' house for the last time. 'No thank you,' she hissed as she proceeded to the door. 'When my son is welcome, I will return.' His grandfather had then said, 'You have made your decision, which we will respect. However, if you ever require financial assistance to educate your child...' His mother had then retorted 'I require nothing from you' and as she left her parents' home for the last time she hissed, 'He is *my* son and I will provide for him. Provide his every emotional and financial need.' They left Kelvinside there and then and they never returned. They settled in Edinburgh and what had always remained a mystery to him was that his mother, who worked as a secretary, had somehow persuaded the Board of George Heriot's School that his father was dead and he was therefore entitled to be educated there on a scholarship basis. Then, to finance his way through his law degree, he had to work part-time as a waiter. To assist him, his mother had taken on an additional job as an evening usherette in the State Cinema in Leith.

Thinking of his mum, and how she had sacrificed for him, which was probably a contributing factor to her early demise, always saddened him. It was good to know she saw him become a competent advocate and that all she had done for him had paid dividends. He knew that it was time to move on. But, he wondered, how could he move on with anyone special if he remained wary about telling them about his past?

Changing the subject he said, 'Look Kitty, may I call you, Kitty?'

'Well yes, but in your class I would probably be known as Katherine.'

The expression that crossed his face caused her to shiver. It was as if she had touched a raw nerve. And when he spoke, she was reminded of how he conducted himself in court. 'Class? Are you aware that people putting so much emphasis on class and social standing is a type of pernicious ailment that destroys and...?' He didn't finish his statement. Kitty was aware that he had dropped his guard, but as soon as he realised, he quickly changed his tone and said, 'Look I have booked myself into that hotel on the cliff top up there.'

Not wishing to cause him any further discomfort, she looked up at the superior building before quipping, 'Now should I not have known that you would have installed yourself there?'

'Bet it is not as homely as your B&B.'

'You're right there. And not only is it the best boarding house around here but you are always assured of a shoulder to cry on if you need it.'

'I hope that won't be necessary today or in the future. But back to what I was saying, I am a resident at the hotel and they serve morning coffee and croissants on the veranda so how about we avail ourselves?'

During morning coffee Felix persuaded Kitty to go with him to see the famous pretty little fishing port of Polperro. Both found the little village enchanting so they stayed on for lunch. The more time they spent together the more they relaxed in each other's company. She was really pleasantly surprised that he was quite an affable fellow and not the stiff and formal stuffed shirt he appeared to be in court.

As for Felix, he couldn't believe that she could take up his full attention and for the first time since he became an advocate his mind was not going over one of his pending cases.

All too soon, for both of them, it was time to leave the magical place that had bewitched them – so much so that they felt so comfortable in each other's company that they wished the day could last forever.

Like people who have known each other for a long time, and are at ease with each other, there were several lapses in the conversation whilst they travelled back. Both were thinking how pleasing it was that they had started to look at each other in different ways.

On arrival back at the Crinnis Beach, Kitty was surprised to see that her deckchair wasn't there. 'I don't believe it,' she exclaimed. 'Surely no one would steal a deckchair. Ah well, if they have I will just have to buy a replacement for Laura.'

Next stop was Laura's home and Kitty had just jumped out of the passenger seat of Felix's car when Laura opened the door.

'Kitty,' she exclaimed, rushing forward to grab hold of her. 'Where on earth did you get to? Exercise class finished early, Mike then picked me up and dropped me down at the beach so you and I could have a lazy lunch together and all I found was the deckchair and your book.' Laura sighed. 'I was so scared. I mean it looked as if you had gone for a swim in the sea and I thought you might have ... well you just might have...'

'Sorry, Laura, I should have left a note.'

By this time Felix was out of the car, and as he stepped forward, he extended his hand to Laura. 'You don't know me but I'm Felix and I am the one to blame for whisking Kitty away.'

Laura made no attempt to shake Felix's hand, and as she stepped back from him she uttered, 'Oh but you are so wrong, Mister Martin, I do know you. For a while you were forever in my nightmares.' She then abruptly turned and re-entered her home.

Kitty was dumbfounded. The Laura who had just spoken to Felix was a Laura that she just didn't know. A Laura she should have known. Why was she so naive to think that all that had happened to Laura and her family, when Eric was charged with murdering Edna, would be something that they would ever get over? Laura had been so much a part of her life, an important part of her life, that she was overwhelmed by a compulsive desire to run after Laura and comfort her.

Without even stopping to give a wave goodbye to Felix, Kitty fled indoors after Laura.

'Laura, what's got into you?'

'Into me, Kitty?' Laura challenged. 'Now I might not be as bright as you but my head doesn't button up the back. So don't try and tell me that you just happened to bump into him on Crinnis Beach and you both remembered each other from Eric's trial away back in September 1945. In case you don't know it, Kitty, it is now May 1949. And he would, in nearly four years, have hung hundreds out to dry, so how come he would remember you?'

'Okay, calm down. Yes I did meet him last week when I was coming out of the prison. Believe me I was as surprised as you are that he remembered me. It was bucketing down and he offered me a lift, which I was glad to accept.'

'I can see that you were.'

Kitty ignored Laura's sarcasm. 'I was in a hurry because I had to catch the morning train for London. I hadn't eaten all day so he offered to treat me to supper.'

'And?'

'Nothing. I told him I was coming to visit you, and see when he turned up on the beach this morning I was ... blown away.'

'Blown away? You sure are. Have you forgotten all that he implied about Eric?' Kitty shook her head. 'Now don't tell me you, who was born in Ferrier Street and reared in Restalrig, think that because you are a qualified staff nurse you can set your cap for him. Professionals like him don't marry lassies like us.'

Kitty found it difficult to do as she had been taught and that was when you were getting angry the best way to cope is not to raise your voice and to breathe in deeply. 'Laura, I hardly know the man. If you had any sense you would have noticed he is much older than I am. We just had a nice little jaunt about together... Seeing sights neither of us had ever seen before. And as to you thinking I am getting above myself, what do you think of a lassie, who had the same upbringing as me, marrying a quantity surveyor?'

Laura was about to retort when Mike came in. Looking from Laura to Kitty he could see both women were not quite themselves. 'Problem?'

'Sorry, Mike, I went off with Felix Martin...'

'Who in the name is Felix Martin?'

'Just the big shot Edinburgh lawyer that stitched our Eric up good and proper.'

'Oh, I remember him. Superior, aloof sort of guy.'

'Not aloof today, he wasn't. And Kitty would like me to believe it was just by chance that he was passing by Crinnis Beach and then like a knight in shining armour he whisked her away in his chariot.'

'Right girls, you two have been friends through thick and thin for how long?'

'Since we were at school.'

'That's right, Kitty. So let's cool everything down. Now, Laura, my love, Kitty came here to spend time with you...' Laura was about to interrupt but Mike silenced her by putting up his hand. 'Tomorrow is Tuesday. That is the day that you said you were going to spend with Kitty. Now the plan was that you would both get your hair done and then go out to lunch. That's not for change. Wednesday well ... we will see what happens and on Thursday Kitty is off home.'

'Yes, I have to get back, I still have not settled on a new job.'

Laura, who had blown up so quickly, was now beginning to calm. 'Sorry, Kitty, it's just that I don't wish to see you getting hurt. That man doesn't care who he wounds.'

Kitty smiled. 'Know something, Laura, I'm a big girl now and no one takes me for a hurl.'

Felix was reading his morning paper in the foyer of the hotel when Mike came in, and when he saw him he went over and, offering his hand, he said, 'I think that you may be Felix Martin?' Felix nodded. 'I am Mike Bailey, Laura's husband.'

'I see. Sorry if I upset your wife yesterday. I do know that by doing my job I appear to be immune to people's suffering. Not the case.' Felix then indicated the chair adjacent to his and signalled that Mike should sit down. When he was seated Mike passed over a letter from Kitty to Felix. After reading the letter Felix nodded. Looking out of the window at the brilliant sunny morning, Felix mused. To Mike's surprise he then said, 'Don't suppose you have time to play some golf this afternoon?'

Thursday morning arrived all too soon. Mike was driving Kitty to the station. Laura, who had boarders to attend to, had to say goodbye to Kitty at the door.

'Kitty, please be careful. Your happiness means so much to me. I just don't want you humiliated again like you were by Dougal McNeill.'

'Laura, I am all the adult that I will ever be. I probably will never ever see Felix Martin again. After all, I did only meet him again last week. Now what you should be doing is looking after yourself and preparing for your baby coming. I will try and get back down to see you nearer your time. It will all depend on what job I get and where I get it.'

The young women embraced and both were near to tears. Mike, leaning over from the driver's seat and shouting, 'Kitty, if you don't get a move on you'll miss the train,' caused Kitty to quickly release Laura before jumping into the passenger seat.

As they travelled along Mike did most of the chatting and he was just asking Kitty how Connie was doing when Kitty's hand flew to her mouth. 'Oh thank you for reminding me. I used your phone last night to speak to Connie. They have a telephone in the house now because my dad needs one for his constituency business.' She rummaged in her bag until she found her purse and fished out a half crown. 'That should cover the charge.'

'I think that's too much.'

'Believe me it was worth four times that just to hear Connie tell me that she is back in love with my dad again.'

'Everything fine then?'

'Until the next crisis.' Kitty giggled, before adding, 'Believe it or not I was just saying to Aunt Kate, who lives on a knife edge with her three children, that we do get rocky times but we always manage to pull together and get through them.'

'Kate's three are settling then?'

'Yes, for now, but as the boys grow into young men who knows what they will do? Israel just might tempt them. But as Aunt Kate says, life is like what it says in the bible ... you get the fat times and the lean times. The one thing for sure is we keep moving on.'

Mike had now driven his car into the side of the

road. 'Right Kitty, time for you to get off.'

Kitty looked about. They were nowhere near the St Austell train station. 'But, Mike, I have to catch the ten o'clock train.'

Mike by now was out of the car and had gone round and lifted her luggage out of the boot. He then proceeded to the car that was parked in front of his. Slinging Kitty's large case into the already open boot he then handed Kitty her small over-night bag.

'What's going on?'

By now Felix had come round to shut the boot.

'Kitty,' Mike said, as he took hold of her by the shoulders, 'It's your life. And believe me I'm not telling you what to do but you and Felix have a long haul home in front of you so it's up to both of you to get yourselves sorted out.'

'But Mike... I've missed my train.'

'Yeah, but you might not have missed the boat.' With these final words Mike grabbed hold of Kitty and kissed her on both cheeks. 'Good luck, Kitty.' With five long strides he was back in his own car.

There was nothing else Kitty could do other than get herself into the passenger seat beside Felix. However, she was further put out when Mike pulled out to pass Felix's car and both of them saluted each other.

'When was all this arranged? I didn't even know that you knew Mike.'

'Amazing what can get sorted out on the golf course. I like Mike. I think, in the near future, he and I will become very good friends ... very good friends indeed.'

Kitty twittered.

'And he will referee any future problems that may arise between you and Laura.'

'You think so?'

'Know so. Now sit back and relax. By the way, we are going to break our journey for the night. I know a lovely little hotel, The Wild Boar, in Bowness-on-Windermere in the Lake District.'

'But I need to go straight home. I intend to look for a job tomorrow. I have to look for a job tomorrow. I can't live on fresh air.'

'Just relax. You will love staying in this hotel. And stop sulking... I am just trying to make it up to you for spoiling your time with Laura.'

On arrival at The Wild Boar, Kitty was impressed. It was one of those little country places that you hoped that, some day, you would be able to stay in. However, as they proceeded to the reception, Felix confided to her that the hotel had lovely rooms with four-poster beds. 'Oh no!' she exclaimed as she drew up abruptly. 'Don't you realise I have never slept with a man!'

He shrugged. 'Oh, give me credit for having worked that one out.'

She ignored his comment. 'And what is further more, as a teenager, I promised my mother I would remain a virgin until my wedding night.'

'I see. But your mother is dead.'

'She is. But a promise is a promise and I will not break my promise to her for anyone. So get along and book two single rooms.'

'No need. I phoned ahead from Carlyon Bay and did just that.'

It was quite late when Kitty got herself into

bed. After the scene she had made when she had insisted on a single room for herself, she tried to make amends. They had had their dinner by the dancing flames of the log fire, and as the heat warmed the chill of the May evening, she relaxed. Felix chatted away, especially about himself, and he confided to her that very soon he would be appointed King's Counsel. He then went on to talk about his looming fortieth birthday. He was quite open about turning forty in June and this admission jolted Kitty. She was just going on twenty-five so her imagining that he was trying to seriously and honourably court her was just so ridiculous. It was true what Laura had said in that Kitty had visions of getting above herself. No way would an advocate, soon to be a King's Counsel, wish to marry a nurse, even if she was a virgin.

Kitty was already sitting in the passenger seat awaiting Felix, who was settling up the bills for the overnight accommodation. It was a lovely sunny day but somehow she felt a chill settling into her bones. This, she knew, was because she was dreading saying goodbye to Felix. Yes, it had been such a lovely time with him, but she very reluctantly accepted that when they arrived home, they would have to go their separate ways.

Once Felix was in the car, he half turned towards her and as he manoeuvred the car backwards out of the parking bay he said, 'Date for your diary. Saturday the 29th October 1949.'

'But I thought you said that your birthday was next month and you were not going to have a party.'

'That's right.'

'So what is so special about Saturday the 29th October 1949?'

'Just that it will be our wedding day and I have booked us a four-poster-bedded suite for our honeymoon.'

'Are you joking?'

'No, never been so serious in my life.' He now turned to face her full on. 'Kitty,' he began as he sought for her hand. 'Now we have found each other again, let's not waste the next few years courting. I love you ... have done so from the day you first spoke to me outside St Giles' Cathedral.' He exhaled before adding, 'And I think, no I know, that you love me. What I am saying is that I am offering to look after you, care for you – spoil you. We have so much going for us ... let's not waste any more time.'

Kitty allowed a moment to elapse before nodding. He smiled. Then after two or three passionate kisses he started to steer the car forward.

Feeling elated, she relaxed back into her seat. And as she settled down for the long haul, she mused, *Isn't it just so wonderful, to be adored by a mature man that you love and wish to spend the rest of your life with?*

The publishers hope that this book has given you enjoyable reading. Large Print Books are especially designed to be as easy to see and hold as possible. If you wish a complete list of our books please ask at your local library or write directly to:

**Magna Large Print Books**
Magna House, Long Preston,
Skipton, North Yorkshire.
BD23 4ND

This Large Print Book for the partially
sighted, who cannot read normal print, is
published under the auspices of

## THE ULVERSCROFT FOUNDATION

### THE ULVERSCROFT FOUNDATION

... we hope that you have enjoyed this
Large Print Book. Please think for a
moment about those people who have
worse eyesight problems than you ... and
are unable to even read or enjoy Large
Print, without great difficulty.

You can help them by sending a
donation, large or small to:

**The Ulverscroft Foundation,
1, The Green, Bradgate Road,
Anstey, Leicestershire, LE7 7FU,
England.**
or request a copy of our brochure for
more details.

The Foundation will use all your help to
assist those people who are handicapped
by various sight problems and need
special attention.

Thank you very much for your help.